Chrissa
Stands Strong

by
Mary Casanova

For my daughter, Kate, who continues to inspire and teach me

Published by American Girl Publishing, Inc.
Copyright © 2009 by American Girl, LLC

Questions or comments? Call 1-800-845-0005, visit our Web site at **americangirl.com**, or write to Customer Service, American Girl, 8400 Fairway Place, Middleton, WI 53562-0497.

Printed in China
09 10 11 12 13 14 LEO 10 9 8 7 6 5 4 3 2 1

Illustrations by Richard Jones

Special thanks to Patti Kelley Criswell, MSW, Dr. Michael Obsatz, and Susan Kovacs

Cataloguing-in-Publication Data available from the Library of Congress.

Contents

1
Back-to-School Shopping

Lake Chandler called to me. Though I usually love shopping with Mom for back-to-school clothes, all I wanted to do this Saturday morning was to get back to the lake. Tryouts for the Edgewater Swim Club were on Monday—only two days away—and I wanted to keep practicing my dives from our swim raft.

As music blared overhead, I pulled on another outfit and then stepped out of the dressing room. In front of a three-panel mirror, I turned this way and that.

"Hey, I tried on that outfit and it looked awful."

The voice sent a twinge from the ends of my hair to my toes. I didn't turn around, but I glanced at the reflection behind my own. It was Tara James—the biggest bully in last year's fourth-grade class.

"But it looks really great on you!" Tara nodded at my reflection.

I smoothed the top across my waist. Tara being nice? I doubted it.

"Honest," she continued, "it's cute."

I forced myself to turn around. Petite and with flashing eyes, Tara wore her usual nothing-can-stop-me

"Hi, Tara," I finally said. "And, um, thanks, I guess."

attitude. In a flash, the second half of fourth grade played over in my head. From the moment I'd arrived as a new student in Mr. Beck's fourth-grade class the day before Valentine's Day, Tara had been unfriendly. More than unfriendly—she'd been *mean*. She and two other girls, sometimes called the Queen Bees and sometimes called the Mean Bees, had played tricks on me and on Gwen, another fourth-grader who had plenty of troubles of her own. And then, when one of the Mean Bees—Sonali—finally left their group because she was tired of their mean pranks, Tara had been furious at me and accused me of stealing Sonali. Now the Mean Bees were down from three to two: just Tara and Jadyn.

"What's the matter? Cat got your tongue?" Tara asked with a teasing smile.

In only a few seconds, my stomach had managed to get as tangled as a ball of yarn after my grandmother's cat has attacked it. But at least Nana's cat attacks only out of playfulness! It's different with Tara. I couldn't be too careful.

"Hi, Tara," I finally said. "And, um, thanks, I guess."

I turned back to the mirror. "So where's Jadyn?" I said to her reflection. It somehow felt safer than talking to her face-to-face.

"She's meeting me here in a little while." Tara turned into a different dressing room and returned with a dress. "Hey, you should try this one. It didn't work on me, but I bet that it'll look great on you."

I hesitated, then accepted the dress. I slipped into my dressing room but in seconds was standing back at the mirror. I was surprised how much I liked it.

"You *have* to get it. It's totally you," Tara said.

Just then, Mom walked back into the dressing room corridor. She had a few more outfits draped across her arm. In the reflection, I saw her shoot a questioning glance at Tara. She knew how hurt I'd been and probably wondered why I would come within a mile of Tara if I didn't have to. Then her gaze shifted to me and my reflection. Her face cleared and she smiled.

"That's adorable on you, Chrissa! I would never have guessed. Let's get that one for sure."

"Um, it wasn't my first choice, but then Tara suggested it. Uh, Mom, you remember Tara?" Mom nodded. "And Tara, this is my mom, Dr. Maxwell."

"Well, Tara," Mom said, studying my reflection again. "It's clear you have an eye for fashion."

"I know." Tara looked pleased. "That's what everybody tells me."

Mom's right eyebrow flicked ever-so-slightly

upward at Tara's outright boastfulness. It made me think of one of Nana's rules: *Don't boast.* Clearly, no one had drilled Tara on that one.

I took one last glance at the dress, which I loved, and headed to my dressing room. "Mom, I think I have enough now. We can go."

"Enough?" Tara mimicked. Then she said in a silly queenly voice, "But a girl can never have enough clothes!"

Mom laughed, and I giggled, too.

After checking out, I followed Mom past racks of shirts and skirts, pants and dresses. Just as we were leaving the store, someone touched my elbow. "Before you leave," Tara said.

I stopped and pivoted.

"We're going to be competing for spots on the swim team," she began.

I braced myself. If I knew Tara, she was probably going to tell me that I didn't have a chance or that I shouldn't even try out, just to give herself an advantage. She had been the best fourth-grade girl swimmer and diver until last year, when I arrived at Edgewater Elementary. It turned out that we were pretty well matched.

"I know things didn't go well last year," she said.

"But this year, things could be different . . . Maybe we could be friends this year."

There was something soft in her eyes and the way she angled her head. She seemed, well . . . sincere.

"Yeah, maybe," I said, cautiously. "That would be good."

As I pushed through the mall doors into the steamy outside air, I passed Jadyn—the other Mean Bee—with her mother a few steps behind her. "Meet you at the Food Court in five," she said into her pink cell phone, then clicked it shut with a snap. I was apparently invisible to her, which was fine with me. A conversation with one Bee was enough for the day.

I still couldn't quite believe what had just happened. I glanced at my shopping bag. In it were not just one—but two—outfits that had come with Tara's compliments. I never would have guessed.

Gwen and Sonali were not going to believe this!

2
New Beginnings

"Hey, Tyler, watch this!"

Perched on the edge of the swim raft, I prepared for another back dive. With my weight on the balls of my feet, I brought my arms down, bent my knees, and pushed off. Clasping my hands in a V over my head, I sliced through the warm air and then disappeared into Lake Chandler.

Yes! The dive felt perfect! I surfaced, wiped water from my eyes, and beamed at my brother. "So, how was that?"

Tyler sat cross-legged on the raft, his eyes hidden beneath his hair, almost like our mini llamas, Cosmos and Checkers, before shearing. "Not bad, Chrissa," he said, "but your feet were three zillion miles apart!"

His words stung. Over the summer, I'd worked on back dives. At first I only back-flopped, but I'd made progress. I swam to the raft's ladder and climbed up. "How can you say that? Maybe you need a haircut so you can see better."

"I can see fine," he said. "And so will the coach. On a scale of ten, you'd be lucky to get a two."

"A two?" I slumped down beside him. "C'mon!"

A light breeze rippled the bay's surface and nudged a half-dozen sailboats in the distance.

Tyler stood. "Remember how you used to pretend you were a mermaid?"

"Yeah."

"Next time," he said, "think of your feet as a mermaid's tail. Keep them glued together like this." He strode to the edge and somersaulted into a forward one-and-a-half.

As he surfaced, he dared me to score him. "That was a ten, wasn't it?"

"Maybe a one," I said, lying. Mom was right. My being eleven months younger than Tyler made us too close in age. I hated to always be outdone by my brother.

"It was good and you know it, Chrissa! You're just jealous!"

"And you're boasting," I said.

As I stood up and prepared to do another dive, he glanced toward shore. "Here comes trouble."

I turned. "Oh, good!" Gwen and Sonali were walking down the dock that jutted out from Nana's big lawn. When we'd moved here in February to live with Nana, I'd had a tough time starting at a new school in the middle of the year, but now that I'd made new friends, I rarely missed my old school anymore.

Sonali walked to the end, pulled her silky hair back into a ponytail, dived, and swam for the raft. Gwen, however, sat and dangled her feet in the water. Her long blonde hair and bangs were pulled back. Despite Tara's friendliness earlier today in the dressing room, I couldn't forget that one of her meanest tricks was when she'd cut off Gwen's bangs in the girls' restroom last March.

"C'mon, Gwen!" I called. "Come join us!"

When Gwen finally jumped in, she did the breaststroke toward us. She wasn't a strong swimmer, but she'd improved a lot over the summer.

Once we were all sitting on the raft, Tyler showed off with another forward one-and-a-half, this time adding a few inches of air to his rotation.

"Wow!" Gwen exclaimed.

"That was awesome!" Sonali added as he surfaced.

I rolled my eyes.

"Cannonball!" I yelled. Sonali, Gwen, and I jumped off the raft at the same time, arms tucked around our legs, and bombarded Tyler.

When the water calmed down again, he hand-slapped the water and sent droplets flying into my face.

"Like I said, you're just jealous!" yelled Tyler.

When it turned into a splashing war of three against one, Tyler headed for shore and called back, "Mission Outta-Here!"

I was ready for some girl time. Besides, I was bursting to tell Sonali and Gwen my news. As we stretched in the sun, I began, "You won't believe what happened this morning!"

"What?" Gwen asked, turning to her stomach and rising on her elbows.

"This morning when I was shopping with my

mom," I began, "I stepped out of the changing room and you won't believe who was there."

"Who?" Sonali asked.

"Tara," I said, and added "and she was actually nice to me—and funny, too."

Sonali said, "Yeah, that's Tara. She can be funny—and even nice, too—when she *wants* something." Her eyebrows scrunched together as if she was doing serious detective thinking. "So, I wonder . . . what does she want?"

"She said she wants to be friends."

"Whoa," Gwen said, jumping up like a jack-in-the-box. "You didn't fall for that, did you?"

"Well, I—um—I think she might have meant it."

My friends looked at me as if I'd lost all my brain cells. I tried to explain exactly what had happened. Then I added, "And she nearly knocked me over when she admitted things didn't go so well last year."

"Huh," Gwen said, crossing her arms across her swim top. "Now that almost makes me laugh."

I pressed on. "She sounded really sincere when she said she'd like to be friends."

Sonali piped up. "I know her. She's still mad that I'm friends with you two and not her anymore. Don't trust her."

I was smart enough to be wary about Tara, but I remembered another of my grandmother's sayings and repeated it to my friends. "Hey, everyone deserves a second chance."

Sonali and Gwen just shook their heads. "Everyone except Tara," Sonali said.

I looked away toward shore. A female mallard and her brood of nine growing ducklings bobbed in and out around the dock. As they dipped their bills underwater, their white rump feathers and webbed feet pointed skyward. Maybe my friends were right. Tara being nice was like turning everything upside down. I probably shouldn't give her a second thought, let alone a second chance. I shouldn't trust her, I decided.

I rose, stepped to the edge of the dock, and dove. But I forgot to keep my feet together, and they hit the water with a stinging slap.

Later, Nana called, "Girls! Cookies and lemonade!"

We wasted no time getting out of the water. Wrapped in beach towels and comparing our wrinkled fingertips, we crossed under the willow tree to the screened gazebo, where a plate of Nana's homemade sugar cookies and a pitcher of lemonade waited atop a floral tablecloth.

"Teatime," Nana said. "Thought you girls might be ready for something to eat by now."

"Thank you, Nana," I said. Sonali and Gwen chimed in their thanks, too.

As we wolfed down cookies, Nana headed out the screen door of the gazebo. "I'm going to leave you young ladies to yourselves. I need to get back to my spinning. There's nothing quite as satisfying as turning a mound of raw fleece into yarn." Then she headed back toward the house, where Mom was working in one of the flower beds and tossing weeds into a mound on the lawn.

While we sat there, Dad and Tyler drove up in the pickup and parked near Dad's pottery studio. Gwen and Sonali looked questioningly at the truck, its box filled with lumber.

"Oh, more stuff for the llama barn," I said. "We're still replacing rotten boards and rebuilding the stalls."

"How long until Cosmos has her baby?" asked Sonali.

"About two weeks," I said. "About the time school starts, so we're trying to finish up fast."

Bling! Bling! Sonali's cell phone sang from her backpack. She rummaged around, found her phone, and flipped it open.

"Text message," she said.

"Who from?" I asked.

She showed us and it read, "Private Number."

Then her eyebrows scrunched up as she scrolled. "Weird," she said and read the message aloud. "It says, "Watch out for Chrissa, the Llama-Faced Girl!"

"Oh, it does not," I said with a laugh.

Then, to prove it, she showed us the text.

If the message hadn't been about me, I might have thought it was funny. "Huh. I'll bet it's from Tyler. He's trying to get back at me."

"For what?" Gwen asked. "For cannonballs?"

I told them about our rivalry and my teasing. "It isn't nice, but he's been bugging me. I mean, he's getting better and better at diving—and he knows it."

"But," Sonali said, studying her cell phone, "if Tyler did this, wouldn't it show your family's name and number? I'd bet this is from Tara."

Gwen fingered her hair. "Sounds like something she might do," she said, reaching for another cookie.

I replayed this morning and how Tara had said she'd like to be friends. My insides twisted around like a giant pretzel. What if this was from Tara and it had all been a show? Was it another mean game of hers? When school started, would she mock the clothes that she'd encouraged me to buy? I chewed on my lower lip. "But she seemed so sincere."

"Tara can *act* nice when she wants to." Sonali wound strands of her long hair around her finger. "You don't know her like I do, Chrissa. I'm not falling for her games, and you shouldn't either. She just doesn't want me to be friends with you."

3

Repairs

Mom hammered the last board in place, stepped back, and examined the new stall. "With Cosmos so close to her due date, it feels good to get the barn finished and ready for our little newcomer."

It was Sunday afternoon, and the llama barn was nearly done. With a new roof and inside walls, it was basically brand-new. Tyler and I had done a little bit of everything: We had used levels to make sure things were straight. We had handed up electric drills, hammers, measuring tapes, and shingles. We had even painted the exterior siding with red stain until our arms ached. Now the barn was ready with four clean and sturdy stalls—one for tack and hay, one for Checkers, one for Cosmos, and one for Cosmos' baby-to-be, after it was weaned.

"I can't wait! And even Gwen and Sonali are excited," I said, leaning on a stall's half door. "Our very own *cria!*" I liked the word for a baby llama. And no matter what color it would turn out to be, it would be adorable because mini llamas are beyond cute.

Then I remembered the mean text message that

had been sent to Sonali's cell phone:

Watch out for Chrissa, the Llama-Faced Girl! I bit down on my lip. As much as I wanted to forget the message, it kept popping into my mind. Who'd sent it? And what had I done to deserve it? I tried for the umpteenth time to push it out of my head.

"Okay, gang," Dad said. "Next we need to replace old posts and fence boards."

"Now?" Tyler groaned. "Can't we take a break first? Tryouts are tomorrow and I need to practice." I nodded in agreement.

Mom gave Dad a look that meant that she sided with us.

Dad laughed. "Okay, Tyler. You and Chrissa have been great. You are officially awarded the rest of the day off. We'll take it from here."

"Woo-hoo!" Tyler exclaimed. "I'm calling Joel!" During our first week at our new school, he and Joel had started arguing at recess about what would happen to a spaceship if it got too close to a black hole. When Joel brought in computer searches and various science articles to prove his theory, their friendship was sealed. Since then, Tyler and Joel had been inseparable.

"Well, I'm calling Gwen and Sonali! If we get to the raft first, it's ours."

"Yeah, right," Tyler replied, racing off to the house. "We'll see about that!"

When the boys claimed the raft first, Sonali, Gwen, and I set off on the paddleboat. The sun sizzled on my shoulders, but they were well-coated with sunscreen under my life vest. Exploring the shoreline, we meandered past our neighbors' docks and under the bridge that separated our bay from a riverbed. Then we turned and pedaled back.

When we came around the cluster of cedars that marked the eastern point of Nana's property—our property—I spotted Tyler and Joel still on the swim raft.

"Our turn!" I called out as we pedaled closer. I noticed a mound underneath a towel and at first thought they'd brought Keefer, Nana's Siamese cat, onto the raft. But that didn't make sense. I mean, Keefer loves to play in sinks and bat at water dripping from a faucet, but I knew he'd hate being on the raft. He *is* a cat, after all.

As we drew close, Tyler yanked the towel off a small mountain of water balloons. "Incoming spacecraft!" he shouted. "Alert! Alert!"

"Enemy invasion!" Joel yelled, launching a balloon at us.

Like giant jelly beans, water-filled balloons soared

toward us and over us.

We shrieked, pushed hard on the pedals, and veered sharply away.

One hit the back of our seat with a *sploosh!* Another hit a pedal—*splash!*—and broke near our feet. Tyler was doubled over, laughing. Joel picked up another balloon.

A stray water balloon floated in our path. "Grab it," I said to Gwen.

She snagged it out of the water and handed it to me with a smile. "Go, Chrissa!"

"This is for sending that message!" I shouted, sitting up higher on the paddleboat seat. I pulled my arm back, kept my eye on Tyler, and let the green water balloon fly. To my amazement, it flew straight toward my target! It hit Tyler's shoulder and burst, tipping him off balance. He teetered and fell backward off the raft and into the lake.

I was stunned by my lucky aim. Gwen and Sonali cheered.

When Tyler surfaced, he shot me a grimace. "Hey, Chrissa! Trying to take out your competition for tomorrow's tryouts?"

I laughed along with Gwen and Sonali as Tyler swam back to the raft, pushed his hair out of his eyes, and yelled, "This calls for intergalactic revenge! Captain Joel, more water missiles!"

We pedaled frantically away, laughing while water balloons rained down around us.

"Joel!" Dad called from shore. "Phone for you! And Tyler, you guys leave the girls alone!"

Later, after dinner, when Tyler went to sleep over at Joel's house, Sonali, Gwen, and I set up the tent. We pitched it in the backyard between the lake and the bonfire. Nana, Dad, and Mom joined us to roast marsh-mallows. As we swatted at mosquitoes, we talked about Cosmos and the cria soon to arrive.

Sonali tilted her head. "I can't wait. I've never seen a baby llama in my whole life before!"

"Me, either," I admitted.

Like fireflies rising toward the sky, sparks lifted from the fire—along with our voices. Mom taught us songs from when she was a camp counselor, and we sang "Barges" and then "Edelweiss" as a round. When one of us made a mistake, we cracked up laughing until Sonali, Gwen, and I were giggling too hard to sing.

Once one person started yawning, everyone did, so we doused the fire with a bucket of water from the lake. Then Sonali, Gwen, and I hurried into the tent, quickly closing the zippered screen behind us. From start to finish, it had been a perfect day.

Settled into our sleeping bags, we talked about school starting soon and swim-team tryouts tomorrow.

"You know, I'm not a strong enough swimmer yet to try out," Gwen said, "but I'm happy to come watch."

"That would be really nice," Sonali said.

"Yeah," I agreed. "Even if we don't make it into the diving division, I'm sure we'll be on the swim team." I paused. "And Tara's so good, she'll be on the team, too. As a team, we're going to have to work together if we want to win. I guess I still have my fingers crossed that Tara wants to change."

At first there was no response from Sonali and Gwen, so I pressed on. "Okay, let's say she *didn't* send that text message and that she really wants to be friends. What if we invited her over sometime, just to see?"

Sonali clicked on her flashlight and pointed it at me. "I have to see your face. I hoped you were kidding, Chrissa, but you're serious, aren't you?"

Blinded, I blinked and looked away. "Hey, I don't completely trust her either. But it would be a way to give her a chance. See if she's sincere, or up to her old tricks."

The flashlight clicked off again.

Gwen sighed. "Count me out, Chrissa. I mean,

my hair is just starting to look a little normal and I'd like to hang onto it."

"Let's put it this way," Sonali added. "If you invite her over, I'll find some excuse not to come. Sorry, but after quitting her group, it would just feel too weird."

Though we were nearly shoulder to shoulder in our sleeping bags, I felt an uneasy distance from my friends. My mind raced. *What if Sonali and Gwen are right—why should I believe Tara? But what if I'm right?*

We stopped talking after that, and cricket song filled the silence between us.

4

Tryouts

"Girls," Mom whispered at our tent door, "I'm leaving, but if you're going to tryouts, you'd better get up now."

Stomach fluttering, I popped up from my sleeping bag. It was Monday! We had to get to the pool before eight o'clock if we were going to be on time for tryouts. We grabbed a little breakfast, brushed our teeth, and hopped on our bikes.

As our tires whirred along the bike trail and the sun filtered through the green canopy, last night's disagreement seemed to float away. There is nothing like a summer morning—it's filled with possibilities for the day ahead. My muscles worked against the pedals and I downshifted as we headed up a slope. We passed yard after yard showing off purple coneflowers, black-eyed Susans, asters, and petunias. The day was going to be good—I could feel it.

As we neared the Community Center, we saw Joel and Tyler biking in from the opposite direction. "Hey," Joel called. "Ready for tryouts?"

"You bet!" I answered.

Tyler didn't say a word to me, so I figured he was still sore at me for my perfect water-balloon hit.

"Honestly," I said as we walked into the center, "that balloon hit you harder than I expected. I didn't know my aim was that good! Sorry."

"Just watch your back," he said with a laugh, and then he disappeared into the boys' locker room with Joel.

Gwen headed straight for the pool. "I'll be watching from the stands. Good luck!"

As Sonali and I changed and stuffed our backpacks into our lockers, I looked for Tara among lots of new faces. The Edgewater Swim Team is made up of kids from grades four through six.

"How many kids make the team?" one girl asked her mother.

"I don't know," the woman answered. "Don't worry. Just do your best."

I smiled to myself. She sounded like Nana. *Just do your best,* Nana would say, *and let the rest take care of itself.* I would do my best but would keep my fingers and toes crossed, too. I expected to make it onto the swim team, but making the diving division was my special goal.

We headed into the brightly lit pool area with its

clear water, huge windows, multiple swim lanes, and familiar chlorine scent—so unlike Lake Chandler. I love swimming in the pool in winter, but in summer I prefer the lake, knowing that I share its shadows with tiny minnows, sunfish, painted turtles, ducks, and geese.

A whistle blew sharply. Our swim coach and former fourth-grade teacher, Mr. Beck, waved us toward the bleachers, as if he were directing traffic. Wrapped in my towel, I sat between Gwen and Sonali.

"Guess what?" Gwen whispered. "I talked to Mr. Beck and he said that if I'm interested, I can be an assistant! I can help keep times and scores and, maybe eventually, try out for the team."

I grinned at her. "That's great!" I hadn't wanted Gwen to feel left out, so this was perfect. The day really *was* going right.

"Okay, swimmers, listen up!"

The pool area quieted.

"I'm Mr. Beck, and some of you know me as a teacher. But I'm also a coach. Here on the team, just call me Coach. Now, as you are all aware, today's tryouts are for the Edgewater Swim Team. We'll get started with nine-year-olds and move our way up to the twelve-year-olds. Swimming will come first, followed by diving." He scanned those in attendance. "I would like to tell you that there's a spot for each and every one of you, but I may have to limit the size of the team. If you don't make the team today, keep practicing and try out again next time. Got it?"

My palms turned sweaty. *Tyler's a good diver. So is Tara. How many other kids here are good divers, too?* I wondered. When Tyler and I practiced from the swim raft, it seemed as if we would be the only two on the team. *But now*—I glanced left and right—*there must be forty kids at tryouts. Yikes!*

The first two hours dragged by slowly. When it was time for ten-year-olds to demonstrate the breast-stroke and backstroke, I felt pretty confident. I went in a straight line and paid extra attention to my form. Although the crawl is my strongest stroke, the breast-stroke is my favorite, and I came in second—neck and neck with Tara, who was first. The butterfly is my least favorite, but I made an attempt at it, even though I'd never master that one in a whole lifetime. But I wasn't alone. Only one swimmer made it from one end of the pool to the other without stopping halfway—Rachel, a girl in Tyler's class.

"Okay, divers, line up!" Coach called out. "And I want it quiet enough to hear a pin drop while someone is diving, got it? No distractions."

About twenty of us lined up near the low diving board. The high dive, Coach said, was only for quali-fied divers. "And after today, we'll know who those divers will be. We'll start with forward dives, then back dives, and then whatever dive you'd like to do that shows off your skills."

I didn't have a third dive up my sleeve. I raised my hand.

"Yes?"

"For our third dive, is it okay to repeat the back dive?"

"Absolutely," he said. "I don't expect that you're all going to have mastered more advanced dives. We'll be able to work on those as a team."

Waiting my turn, my heart thrummed in my throat, and I shivered. To keep myself calm, I repeated Nana's words to myself: *Just do your best and let the rest take care of itself.*

Tara and Jadyn were ahead of Tyler, Joel, Sonali, and me by about six people. If I'd been standing closer,

I might have risked whispering "Good luck" to Tara, just to be nice. But then I thought of the text message. Maybe it was better to play it safe. I glanced toward the stands, where I knew Gwen was silently cheering me on.

My front dive went by so fast, I honestly wondered if my feet had even been on the board. But when I surfaced, Gwen waved and gave me two thumbs up. I smiled back.

All too soon, we were doing our back dives. Tara climbed up onto the diving board. Head high and shoulders back, she walked confidently toward the end. She pivoted, found her balance, and then pushed up and off. Her body arched and she hit the water almost perfectly, except that her feet were wide apart.

I made a mental note: *Remember your mermaid tail.*

Tyler's dive was perfect. When he climbed out, he shook his head free of water, just like a dog.

I inhaled deeply. This was it. I stepped up the diving-platform ladder and walked to the end of the board, feeling its sandpapery surface beneath my bare feet. When I pivoted, I pictured myself as a beautiful mermaid, more comfortable in water than on land. Then I brought my arms down, pushed off, and imagined my legs and feet as one graceful, shimmery tail.

In a flash I was underwater, pushing toward air.

I imagined my legs and feet as one graceful, shimmery tail.

When I surfaced, Tyler's smile told me I'd done fine. And at that moment, I *knew* he hadn't sent the text. I grinned back.

For my third dive, I repeated my back dive with the same results. As soon as the diving tryouts ended, Coach announced, "Shower up and get dressed. I'll post the results at the reception desk tomorrow. You can check for them tomorrow morning after nine o'clock."

As we made our way to the locker room, Tara shouldered up near me. I flinched, out of habit. "Oh, hi," I said.

"I want to be mad at you!" she started.

I pulled away, but then she used her grand and silly voice again. "No, dear, you don't understand!" Then, in her regular voice, she said, "Chrissa, your dives were really good. I'm used to getting what I want, and so I really, really want to be mad, but—even more, I just want to be friends."

Then she hurried ahead to catch up with Jadyn. I wished that Sonali and Gwen had been there to hear her exact words. There hadn't been a hint of meanness. In our corner of the locker room, I filled them in. "See? She really is trying to be nice. Things seem different with her. I think she's changing."

Gwen wouldn't meet my eyes.

Sonali slowly shook her head. "Chrissa."

I got dressed quickly, frustrated that they wouldn't at least try to see new possibilities. "Meet you outside," I finally said.

5

Shifting Breezes

The next morning, Gwen, Sonali, and I met up early and biked down the winding road as fast as our legs could pedal. I couldn't wait to find out the results of yesterday's tryouts. Breathless, we hurried inside the Community Center. True to his word, Coach had posted the tryout results next to the reception desk. Tyler and Joel were already there. They'd beaten us by about a half-minute.

"We made the swim team—*and* the diving division!" Tyler said, shooting his fist in the air, then high-fiving with Joel. "Excellent!"

I didn't know if "we" meant just him and Joel, or if it included me. I stepped up and ran my finger along the list of names. Not only had I made the swim team, but my name was under the heading of "Divers," too. I couldn't stop smiling. "And there you are, too, Sonali! And look who is listed as assistant manager!"

Gwen stepped closer. "Hey, that's me! Cool."

Sonali gave a little cheer for the three of us. Then she ran her finger down the list of names. "And Tara and Jadyn are divers, too." She shrugged. "Oh well, we'll have to make the best of it."

As we biked back home together, I silently hoped that this would be the start of new friendships—possibly including Tara and Jadyn. It was still a long shot, but maybe by being part of a team, everyone would learn to get along.

That afternoon we took out the small sailboat, but the breeze was fickle, playing games as it switched from one direction to the next. Just when the sail filled, it wilted again as the wind shifted. Now that I was ten and had proved I understood sailing basics, Mom and Dad let me go out as long as I stayed in our bay—and everyone wore a life vest.

"Come about!" I called out, pushing the rudder hard to the left. As we tacked and switched direction, the boom—the long horizontal pole that secured the bottom edge of the sail—swung right. Sonali ducked just in time and joined Gwen on the other side, counter-balancing the gust that now filled the sail.

"Trying to get rid of us, Chrissa?" Gwen asked with a laugh.

"No, I would never try to knock you out of the boat!" I answered.

"Yeah, not like someone we know," Sonali said. "Tara's like that boom."

"The boom?" I repeated.

"Well, you're just moving along," she explained, "thinking everything is fine, and then—*boom!*—Tara clobbers you."

Gwen laughed. "Maybe we should call her Boom-Boom."

I thought of how different Tara had been with me lately. Though I wanted to be part of their fun, I couldn't go along with their joking. "Let's not call her names."

Gwen and Sonali looked at each other.

"Boom-Boom is actually a *kind* name for Tara," Sonali said. "Believe me, I've heard her call others far worse names."

"That's for sure," Gwen added.

Sonali continued, "Come on, you *know* how Tara is, Chrissa. I can't believe you're going soft on her."

Just then, the breeze shifted, the sail drooped, and the boom swung wide.

"Watch out!" I cried. But it was too late.

The sudden movement of the boom sent Gwen and Sonali toppling backward into the water. I glanced back, relieved that they were wearing life vests.

"Wait!" I yelled, trying to handle the rudder and the line for the sail. "I'll tack and come back for you!"

Gwen was sputtering and coughing, but laughing. Sonali yelled, "We'll just swim back! It's close."

Buoyed by their life vests, they swam toward shore. I brought the sailboat back around. By the time I changed directions, my friends were already past the swim raft. But because of the direction of the breeze, I had to angle my way back in, making several tacks back and forth to get closer.

After what seemed like forever, I finally eased the sailboat toward the dock. Tyler and Joel stood ready to help catch the bow. As they did, I quickly released the mainsail and lowered it. Then I glanced around for Sonali and Gwen. "Where'd they go?" I asked.

"They had to get home," said Joel. "Gwen's mom called and then came to pick her up for a dentist appointment. They said to tell you good-bye. "

"Oh."

After Tyler and Joel helped me pull the sailboat up on shore, they ran to the end of the dock and dove, swimming for the raft as if they didn't have a care in the world. Boys, it seemed at times, got along easier than girls.

I gazed out at Lake Chandler. My bare feet were planted in green grass, but I felt as if I were on a sailboat on a windless day. Stranded.

6

Taking Sides

On Thursday afternoon, I joined Nana for tea in the gazebo. I felt like a royal lady, sipping iced tea and reading while Tyler and Joel cannonballed each other from the swim raft. I skimmed the pages of one of Nana's books, called *Raising Llamas Right*. The more I read about the birth process, the more I wondered if Cosmos might give birth at any second. "Nana, Cosmos looks like she's ready to burst, doesn't she?"

"Yes, she sure does."

"Well, it says here that the gestation period is from 335 to 365 days, with the average being 350 days. So that means our cria could come early or late. What if it's early?"

"We won't know," Nana said, "until the time comes. This humidity is hard on Cosmos, though, so she may indeed go early."

"Nana," I said, "when we're done with our tea, could we move the llamas to the new barn? I think it's time that Cosmos gets comfortable with her new surroundings."

"But weren't we going to wait until the barn is

completely finished before moving them?"

"It's *nearly* done, Nana."

She smiled at me. "You sound like a worried mother. If it would help ease your worries, we can show them their new quarters immediately."

"Good!"

While we'd worked over the summer, we'd kept Checkers and Cosmos in a lean-to shelter behind Dad's pottery studio. As we neared their temporary enclosure, up came their heads to stare at us curiously.

"Big day!" I announced, hooking a lead rope to Cosmos' halter. "You're going to love your new home." Cosmos flicked her banana-shaped ears as she waddled, wide with her baby.

Nana and Checkers led the way. "What do you think, girls?" Nana asked, leading Checkers into her new stall with its pine-scented boards.

In the barn's amber glow, I led Cosmos to her stall. The floor was freshly covered with straw. Cosmos sniffed the new boards and bedding with suspicion.

"Don't worry, Cosmos. You'll get used to a new home. I did." And it was true. I really had come to feel that living with Nana here on Lake Chandler was *home*, something I'd never dreamed possible last February, when we'd moved here.

Cosmos' stall was two stalls wide, because the dividing wall was removable and Dad had already taken it out. This way, until the cria was weaned at six months, the mother and baby would have more room—and it would protect the baby from any unwanted kicks from Checkers. Llamas sometimes kick at each other and a kick could be dangerous for a baby. I couldn't wait for the birth and hoped that I wouldn't miss it by being at swim practice or, in another two weeks, at school.

The sunlight coming from the barn door flickered with shadow. I turned.

"Chrissa? Are you in here?"

"Hi, Gwen! Come on in." I stepped out of Cosmos' stall, bolted the half-door, and met Gwen as she entered the barn.

"This is as cute as a dollhouse," Gwen said, her brown eyes shining with approval.

I smiled. "Well, nothing's too good for the baby," I said, repeating something Dad had said when we were working on the barn.

"Your llamas are lucky," she said. "This is pretty nice."

I thought of how Gwen and her mom had been homeless before going to the Sunrise House—and before getting their own apartment. I couldn't imagine how awful that must have been: Not having a bed. Sleeping in their car. Over the past few months she'd shared a few details. Mostly, she said, it was a time that she'd like to forget, a time that still gave her nightmares—even though she and her mom were happy in their new apartment.

Nana interrupted my thoughts. "These llamas are spoiled rotten, Gwen. But in return, they give me fleece to spin and extra chores to do. And they make me laugh. Well, Chrissa, now that you have some company, I'm going in for a nap. Will you and Gwen take the girls back outside when you're done here?"

"Sure, Nana."

As Gwen and I leaned over Cosmos' stall door together, she said, "Cosmos is getting huge!"

"I know. I looks like she swallowed a dozen watermelon seeds and they just keep growing!"

Gwen giggled, and I was glad she was there with me. I'd felt abandoned the other afternoon after sailing, but now my hurt feelings evaporated. Everything seemed fine.

We talked about the llamas, and then about the swim meets ahead and Coach's plan for two unstoppable relay teams. "Chrissa, the coach talks to himself," said Gwen. "I hear what he's thinking lots of times. I think he's going to put you on the relay team."

"But I'm only going into fifth grade."

"You have strong times in the crawl and breaststroke, and fast kick turns."

"Think so?"

Gwen nodded. "The coach thinks so, too. And he'll probably put Tara and Sonali on the relay team, too. He says Sonali's backstroke is awesome."

"Well, he's right. And he sure knows how to pick the right assistant. Keeping track of everyone's times must be hard!"

A tinge of pink crept up Gwen's cheeks.

The barn door creaked and someone else stepped inside. "Hi, Chrissa. Your dad told me I'd probably find you here." It was Sonali, her hair swooshing in a long ponytail as she strode toward us. "Oh, hi, Gwen! I didn't know you were here, too."

She stopped abruptly in front of us, her face strained. "Listen, sorry to just jump in, but I have to tell you guys something."

"This doesn't sound good." I stepped closer, bracing myself for news of another mean text message about me. "What is it?"

Sonali's lower lip quivered. "Now someone has

posted really mean things about *me* online."

"You? Where online?"

"Well," she said, "you know that Web site for the swim team? Coach said to go there to check announcements and other news on the swim team's bulletin board. And that we could all post things on the message board—"

"Yeah?" I said.

"Well, I checked it today. And . . . it's terrible!" The rims of her eyes were red.

Gwen put her hand on Sonali's shoulder. "Sonali, what does it say?"

Trying to hold back tears, Sonali began, "Someone wrote in and said I have a terrible disease that might infect other swimmers . . ." Her voice wobbled. ". . . and that I should be kept out of the pool. Forever!" She pressed her lips together as if to keep from crying, and then she said, "It *has* to be Tara."

Checkers kicked at one of the stall boards, and I turned. "Settle down," I said. "I'll put you back outside in a bit." Then I spun back to Sonali. Tears brimmed in her brown eyes. "Oh, Sonali. That's awful! I feel terrible for you!" I gave her a hug and then said, "But as cruel as this is, it doesn't mean Tara is behind it."

"Chrissa, who else would do such a thing?" she

snapped, tears rolling down her cheeks.

"It's just that," I began, "well, shouldn't we report this and try to find out first where it's coming from, *before* accusing anyone?"

"I think," Gwen said, crossing her arms, "that if you saw a fox leaving a henhouse and then discovered that eggs were missing, what would you say? Tara's already proved what she's capable of doing. Did you forget everything that happened last year? And, when you tell, she just gets worse. And sneakier."

"It *could* be Tara; I know that it could. But I'm just saying we don't have any proof yet."

Sonali wiped away her tears. "You're really defending Tara? She's nice to you a couple times, and now you're on her side? Be careful, because you might be getting poisoned by her. Just like I was. I *know* what she's like, Chrissa—how she can convince you to believe things, do things. She's really mean and really tricky."

I wanted to agree, just to make things easy, but a flickering flame inside me still hoped Tara was changing. "Sonali, I'm just saying that we don't know yet who's doing these things. It *could* be someone else."

Sonali coiled her hair around and around her finger. When she stopped, she turned to me and said, "I thought you'd understand, Chrissa, but I guess I was wrong." Then she looked to Gwen. "Maybe we need a little break from Chrissa for a while."

Gwen looked at me, nodding her head ever so slightly.

"What does that mean?" I asked, my eyes filling with tears.

Gwen hesitated. "Sometimes my mom and I take time-outs from each other, when we're not getting along. Sometimes it helps."

"But—" I stopped, not knowing what to say.

But Gwen and Sonali just turned and walked away, out of the barn and into the harsh sunlight.

7

Tangles

I hid for a few hours in my bedroom, crying into my pillow. Everything was getting so tangled. I didn't want to be pitted against Gwen and Sonali. We were supposed to be *friends*. Friends talk and work things out. Friends don't just walk away.

Finally, I got up. In the mirror, my unhappy reflection looked like someone else's. I splashed cold water on my face in the bathroom, trying to get rid of the red blotches and puffiness. I wanted to go back into my bedroom and just stay there, but I knew I couldn't sulk around forever. I had a decision to make—either go along with Gwen and Sonali, or back up my hunch about Tara. I ran a brush through my hair, then slipped down the staircase.

The house was quiet. I figured everyone was either by the lake or with the llamas. At the entryway table, I thumbed through the phone book until I found what I hoped was Tara's number. Fingers trembling, I dialed Nana's ancient rotary phone, held the heavy black receiver to my ear, and waited. *One ring, two rings* . . . Maybe it would be better if no one answered.

I mean, what if I was wrong and was inviting more trouble by calling? *Three rings* . . . Tara did have a way of turning people into her puppets. Maybe I was playing right into one of her games, and she was pulling the strings to make me dance. Already, Sonali and Gwen were disagreeing with me. Was that part of Tara's plan?

"Hello?" It was definitely Tara. "Hello?"

I almost hung up. For a moment, I couldn't find my voice. "Tara, this is Chrissa, and though I know we got off—"

"Oh. Are you calling about the relay team?" she said, interrupting me. "I heard rumors that Coach might put us on the same team. I should probably swim anchor, though. You know, they put the strongest swimmer last, and—"

There she went again. Bragging. Always having to be the best. Between Tara and Tyler, it was hard to stomach.

The conversation wasn't going the way I'd hoped.

"The reason I called, Tara," I said, interrupting her, "is I've been thinking about what you said. I know we got off to a bad start last year, but let's make this year different. We're on the same swim team now, and well . . ." My heart started hammering. If I hung up now, I'd be playing it safe. But that wouldn't bring Gwen and Sonali back. I'd still be alone. And I'd never know for sure about Tara. "Um, I was wondering . . . would you like to come over sometime? We can go swimming and maybe even practice our dives."

"Really?" Tara replied, sounding surprised and pleased. "That would be great! When?"

"Tomorrow? After practice?"

"Sure, but . . ." she hesitated, "will Sonali and Gwen be there, too?"

My stomach twisted like a strand of red licorice. Tears sprang to my eyes, and I was glad we were on the phone, not face to face. "No. They're not happy with me right now. I guess we're sort of taking a break from each other."

"Oh," Tara said. "Well, maybe that's better, because I don't think they like me all that much. Can't blame them, I guess. Don't tell them I'm coming over, huh?"

I flinched inside. I didn't want to put myself in the middle of Tara and my friends. That wasn't my goal, even though I knew that inviting Tara over would upset them. On the other hand, they'd hurt my feelings. So, was I getting back at them? I didn't think so, but suddenly I wasn't sure. Yet what was I supposed to do?

Spend the rest of summer vacation and the new school year alone? And never give Tara a chance?

"Uh, Chrissa? Are you still there?" Tara asked. Then she said, "Hang on a second." Through the phone I could hear her muffled conversation. "Chrissa, I can't come over tomorrow. My mom says I have to do some errands with her, but I can come over on Saturday."

The way Gwen and Sonali had abandoned me in the barn, I didn't figure they'd be coming over any time soon. "Good," I replied.

"Chrissa!" Mom whispered in my ear as she shook my shoulder Saturday morning. "Wake up! Cosmos is getting close!"

I glanced at my clock, which read 10:36, later than I'd ever slept. I flew out of bed, changed as fast as my legs and arms could move, and raced across the lawn to the barn. Tyler was ahead of me by several strides.

When we entered the barn, Nana, Dad, and Mom were gathered at the edge of Cosmos' stall. Mom and

Dad held coffee mugs and Nana had a travel mug, no doubt filled with tea. I had the sense they'd been hovering for some time.

"Looks like we moved her here just in time, " Nana said, patting my shoulder. "You were right, Chrissa." Outside the stall door, an emergency medical kit was ready, in case of complications. Knowing Mom was a doctor helped me stay calm.

Cosmos was standing with her head against the stall's far wall, as if for support. She breathed heavily, her flanks moving in and out.

Time seemed to stop. We spoke in hushed voices but mostly just watched and waited. Finally, one tiny hoof appeared, then two. Front legs followed.

Cosmos glanced back, as if to check on progress; then she pressed her head against the boards again. Inch by slow inch, a fully formed baby llama eased toward the straw.

"Should we catch it before it drops?" Tyler whispered.

"Unlike horses," I explained, feeling smug for having read up on the subject, "llamas give birth standing. Their babies hang like this for a bit. It helps clear the cria's nasal passage and lungs of fluid."

Nana tightened her arm around my shoulder.

I could tell she was pleased that I'd learned something.

"Don't worry," Nana added. "It's all going just fine."

And Nana was right. The cria, covered by a wet film, slipped onto the straw without injury. I held my breath, waiting for it to breathe. Then it wiggled and snorted, clearly alive. I laughed out loud.

Just like magic—only better. This was real.

Cosmos shifted around, leaned her head toward her newborn, snuffled it, and hummed as she licked its nostrils clean.

Skinny and wet, the cria shook its head and took a snuffly breath. Then it wobbily pushed up on its back legs first, and then on its front legs, until it was standing in a straddled position in the straw. It found its way to Cosmos' belly and immediately started nursing.

Dad glanced at his watch. "A half-hour, from start to finish. That was fast!"

"About average for llamas," Nana said.

I glanced at Mom and Nana, who were both teary-eyed. I laughed. "Why are you crying? We should be celebrating!"

"Whisper, remember?" Mom said. "We don't want to startle them."

"Woo-hoo!" Tyler said quietly.

Dad said in a hushed voice, "Looks like we have another girl in the family!"

"So what are we going to name our little cria?" Nana asked.

"It should be something cosmic," Tyler said, leaning on the stall boards, his chin resting on his crossed arms.

"Hey, how about Starburst?" I suggested. "After all, she did just burst onto the scene."

"That's good, Chrissa," Dad said.

Just then, someone else entered the barn. When I turned, I was startled to see Tara. "Chrissa, hi!" she nearly shouted. "No one answered at the front door, so I—"

"*Shhh!*" we all said at once. I waved her closer and smiled at her reassuringly. "You came at the perfect time. We have a new cria!"

She seemed a little unsure about entering into our cozy cluster around the stall, but the moment she saw the cria at its mother's side, she grinned from ear to ear.

I wished that Sonali and Gwen could share in this moment, too.

Their loss.

But mine, too.

♥

We stayed watching a while longer, until Nana announced that we should give the new mother and baby "a little alone time."

"Besides," Mom added, "it's nearly time for lunch."

After sloppy Joes at the picnic table, and after I'd given Tara a tour of Nana's big house, we ran into Tyler shooting hoops by the garage.

"It's hot! Let's go swimming," Tyler said.

In no time at all, he and Tara and I were on the raft, taking turns diving under a sizzling sun. It felt good to be with them and out of my gloomy mood. Sometimes life is amazing in how different each day can be. Yesterday we had two mini llamas, and now we have three! One day you can have an enemy and the next day a possible new friend. That's why I have to agree with Nana's most often-repeated saying, *Never lose hope.* No matter how dark things might look one day, the next day might be filled with sunny possibilities.

After executing a nearly perfect forward one-and-a-half, Tyler popped up, his wet hair in his eyes. "Olympics, here I come!" he crowed. "Can't you just hear the crowds cheering?"

"Yeah, right," I teased. "It wasn't bad, exactly, but that dive wouldn't get you a top score from any judge."

Tara laughed along with me.

Tyler swam to the ladder and climbed up. "Okay, Chrissa, you're so confident, let's see what you can do next. At least I'm trying new dives. Got anything to show yet besides a back dive?"

That shut me up. I hadn't had the same urge as he had to practice the new dives that the coach had been teaching us. Some of them just seemed too scary— like the inward and the reverse, for starters. I mean, what if I didn't clear the diving board? And I sure wasn't going to try anything fancy on the swim raft with only two feet of clearance from raft to water.

"It's not always the fancy dives that win," I said, repeating the coach's words. He'd told us that simple dives done well bring in points for a team. It's just that the more complicated dives are given more weight, even if they aren't mastered perfectly. I knew I'd eventually try harder dives, but the truth was, I was starting to enjoy competitive swimming more than competitive diving. For Tyler, it was the other way around.

Roaring past us, a speedboat pulling a wakeboarder sent a series of waves toward the raft. We rode out the waves as they lifted the raft up and down and finally settled on shore.

Tara went next. She positioned herself at the edge and readied herself for a back dive. She pushed off, flew a little farther out than she probably wanted, but still managed to go headfirst into the lake.

"I'd give you a four," Tyler said when she came up from underwater.

"A four point seven," I said, just to outscore his scoring.

We dove and swam all afternoon. With a little prodding from Tyler and Tara, I worked up enough courage to try a forward one-and-a-half, with less-than-perfect results.

When I climbed up onto the raft, my belly was red from smacking.

"Way to go," Tyler said. "But at least you tried."

I could feel my irritation with him growing.

"Now, I'll show you how it's really done," Tyler said, perching at the edge, shoulders back and head high. He jumped, and I couldn't help myself. Just as he started, I called out, "Big Head!"

Tara laughed.

I could tell he was attempting a pike, but he didn't have enough air to open up fully, so instead he came down in the water in a royal belly flop.

"Ouch!" Tara giggled. "That one hurt."

When Tyler broke through the surface, he splashed at us. "I would have aced that one if it hadn't been for you, Chrissa."

"At least you're trying," I said, mimicking his words to me.

He rolled his eyes at me. "Guess I have better things to do." He swam toward shore.

I watched him leave with satisfaction. Then I caught myself. Why was I forcing him away when we really had been having fun? Was Sonali right? Was I becoming poisoned by Tara?

I stretched belly-down on the raft and pretended to rest. Head tucked in my arms, I didn't want to meet Tara's eyes.

That evening, after Tara had gone home, Nana called to me upstairs. "Phone's for you, Chrissa!"

I zipped down the stairs, expecting Tara to be on the other end to tell me what a great day she'd had.

Instead, it was Sonali.

"Oh, hi!" I said, glad that she'd let only a few days—not years—go by before getting back in touch. And then I burst out with news I knew she'd like to hear. "Guess what? Cosmos had a baby girl! And we named her Starburst!" I didn't know how to tell her about Tara, so it all came out in a rush. "And . . . Tara came over today, too, and that went really well."

There was a long pause. Then Sonali said quietly, "You mean Tara was the first one to see the baby?"

"I'm sorry. I know you wanted to be here—I really wanted you to be here, too, but . . . well, it all happened so fast."

"You could have called."

"I figured you wouldn't want to be here if Tara was here."

"Well, that's true."

"But, Sonali, you can come over tomorrow to see the baby. Honestly, she's the cutest thing you've ever seen."

Again, there was silence—chilly as a block of ice.

"We'll see," she said. And then she hung up.

8

Dark, Dreary, Dismal Day

A dreary, dismal rain started before I went to bed, and it fell all Sunday morning. After church and lunch, while the rest of my family ran errands, I stepped into what used to be Grandpa's library. It has wall-to-wall bookshelves filled with everything from medical books to Greek mythology to tattered picture books from Mom's childhood. The library still smells of Grandpa's pipe tobacco, and I could almost feel his presence. The computer screen saver glowed, casting an eerie light into the darkened room. I plopped in the padded leather swivel chair, touched the keyboard, and checked to see if I had any new e-mail messages.

"Good!" I said aloud. To my relief, there were e-mails from both Sonali and Gwen. "I bet they want to come over to see Starburst!"

But when I opened their messages, my heart sank. There wasn't a word about meeting our new cria. Instead, they were both mad as yellow jackets about Tara. They also mentioned some mean spam e-mails that seemed to have been sent to everyone on the swim team and were even posted on the swim-team message board.

I looked at the spam e-mails and then at the swim-team message board. One nameless sender had written, "Gwen should get her head examined. What's she doing being the coach's assistant? She can't even add 2 + 2!"

And another said, "Somebody should tell Sonali to cut off her ugly, long hair. Doesn't she know that it could get caught in a pool drain?"

I toggled back to the flurry of e-mails between and from Gwen and Sonali.

The most recent e-mail from Sonali concluded, "Chrissa, it has to be Tara! Or if it's not, then maybe she got *you* to do it—because I notice there's nothing about you. I tried to warn you, but you wouldn't listen. You should NOT trust her!"

I bit hard on my lip and held back tears. This was such a mess! How could they think that I would post anything like that online? Giving Tara a chance didn't mean that I would do something like this to them—or to anyone. They were my friends.

But now they didn't trust me.

Everything about this was so awful—and so unfair! Sweat beaded on my hairline and I thought I was going to throw up.

I replied to both of them at the same time with an IM—an Instant Message—my fingers pounding on the keyboard. "I don't know who did this, but I've never said anything bad about you two. I never would! I never will. You just have to believe me." I pressed SEND.

An IM shot back immediately from Sonali. "It's hard to know what to believe anymore."

And then a message came through from Gwen, too. "I agree. I don't think you would do this, Chrissa, but I don't trust Tara."

I paused, wondering what to write next. But really, what could I say to change their minds? Nothing. Then I started to wonder: How could you find out who was sending the mean e-mails? And the message-board postings—didn't the coach see them? If I told Mom and Dad about this, would they even know what to do? And what if it *was* Tara sending these messages? How did she do it? For what felt like hours, I sat there staring at the screen until the screen-saver images made me dizzy and my stomach started to ache. Finally, I turned off the computer and pushed the chair back.

I yanked on my raincoat and rain boots and dashed past puddles in the grassy lawn. Earthworms slithered, forced aboveground by the rain. Two fat robins hopped along. One paused beside the base of the birdbath, plucked a worm, and flew off with its catch. "Huh," I muttered. I felt like that earthworm.

In the barn, I hung up my dripping raincoat on a wooden peg and walked past Checkers, who was chewing her cud. "You look happy to be inside," I said. Nana had asked Tyler and me to bring in the llamas last night when the first raindrops began to fall. Nana generally likes them to be outside in the paddock during the day and inside at night so that she can sleep without worrying about them, especially now that Starburst has arrived.

Cosmos, the proud mother, was *kushing*— resting with her legs tucked beneath her. I stepped carefully into Cosmos and Starburst's stall and handed Cosmos some hay. Starburst danced away from me but then stopped, gazing at me curiously, her ears perked upright. Her black eyes sparkled with mischief. "Will you let me pick you up?" I asked softly. Though I'd held her a couple of times already, I hadn't picked her up on my own.

Carefully, I moved closer and then I sank down into the straw. Starburst jumped to the left and then stood still. "I won't hurt you," I cooed. She came back

and let me gather her onto my lap. I held her close to my chest and pressed my nose into her coat. "Starburst, you're so lucky," I whispered. "You don't have to deal with girlfriend problems. Llamas might spit at each other when they're angry, but at least you know where it's coming from."

Tears finally came, and I cried into Starburst's soft coat.

In my whole life, I'd never felt so terribly alone.

9

Teamwork

That night at dinner, I was too upset to eat—even Dad's special spaghetti and meatballs.

"Sweetie, what's wrong?" Dad asked. "You've hardly touched your dinner."

I wanted to tell him what had been going on—after all, when things went wrong last spring at school, telling Mom had been helpful. It led to a change in seating arrangements, and things were better after that. But this time was different. Last spring, I *knew* who was causing problems. This time, if I spoke up, I might get the wrong person in trouble. I didn't have an ounce of proof yet. And until I did, I was going to have to go it alone.

"Sorry, Dad, but I don't feel so hot. I'm trying to work something out, but I'm not ready to talk about it."

Dad looked at me closely. "Well, I'm here when you *are* ready to talk about it."

I excused myself and climbed into bed early. I shifted this way and that, hoping to fall asleep so that I could quit playing the mean messages and botched conversations over and over. My head hurt, my

stomach churned, and sometime in the middle of the
night, when everyone was sleeping, I threw up in the
bathroom. I tried to be as silent as I could, hoping no
one would wake up and check on me. I didn't want to
have to talk.

When morning came, the sun was way too bright
and cheery. I rolled over in bed and hid my head under
my pillow, dreading practice. How was I going to deal
with seeing Gwen, Sonali, and Tara at the same time?
How was I going to manage being around all of them in
the locker room and the pool? If only I could swim and
dive with my eyes closed.

But then Tyler was at my door. "C'mon, Chrissa!
Joel can't make it to practice today. Want to bike over
together?" He obviously hadn't seen the message board.

Somehow, having one person on my side—even
Tyler—helped me to climb out from under my covers.

The whole way over, I really wanted to talk about
what had been going on, but I didn't want to start crying again. We locked our bikes in the bike stand, and
walked toward the center's doors. "Chrissa," he said,
"I think I should aim for being an Olympic diver first,
and then, after that, go to work for the space program."

I snapped at him. "Olympics? Wow, Tyler,
with all your bragging lately, maybe I should call you

'Big Head' all the time."

He strode ahead and said over his shoulder, "Boy, are you ever crabby this morning!"

Before I could apologize, he disappeared into the boys' locker room.

I really hadn't meant to be so snotty to him. I didn't even know why I did it. True, he'd been bugging me, but it wasn't fair to take out my other frustrations on him. I couldn't seem to say or do anything right lately.

In the locker room, with my head down, I passed Tara and Jadyn.

"Morning, Chrissa!" Tara called.

"Hi," I said softly, not stopping.

"How's Starburst doing?"

"Fine," I said without enthusiasm, turning to the emptiest corner of the locker room. I opened the locker door and swung my backpack in, but it crashed against the metal door, sounding as if I'd slammed it.

In the background, Jadyn asked, "What's with her today? And who's Starburst?"

"Their new baby llama."

I thought of the mean e-mails. *Was it Tara who had sent those? Why should I trust her?* And now Sonali and Gwen believed the worst—that I might have sent them.

All I wanted to do was to protect myself, to close up as tight as a clam so that no one could get to me. No wonder people use the expression "clamming up." That's exactly what I wanted to do—close up my hard shell around my feelings and sink down through the water, deep into the mud where no one could ever find me. Or ever hurt me again.

That morning, when Coach gave us his regular pep talk, I sat on the first row of bleachers—alone. Tara and Jadyn were behind me to my left. Sonali and Gwen were off to my right. I pretended not to know anyone. It seemed to be the only thing I could do. But acting like a clam hurt. The more I tried to bury my feelings, the more my chest ached. And the more my chest ached, the more my throat dried up. I could barely swallow.

"Before we get started," Coach said, "let me remind you that the swim-team message board will *not* be used to send mean messages or bad jokes like those I saw this weekend. There's a word for using technology this way. Anyone know what it is?" While waiting for an answer, he clasped his hands behind his back and walked back and forth past the front row. "It's called *cyber-bullying*. And I'm not going to tolerate it. If I catch wind of whoever is behind the messages that showed up on the swim club's board, they will face a penalty."

He stopped and looked across the stands at us. "Is that clear?"

Everyone nodded.

"From now on, I will review all messages before they're posted. If anything else like this happens, the site comes down. You're teammates, and this is totally unacceptable in every way." He let his words soak in. "Am I clear?"

Heads nodded again, and a murmur of "Yes, Coach" went up.

"Okay, then. This morning, I've compiled a list of relay teams," Coach announced. He read them off, and to my dread, he'd put Sonali, Tara, and me on the same four-person relay team, along with the red-headed sixth-grader named Rachel. "And the key word is 'team.' If you think only of your own time and your own fame, you'll bring your team down. You must learn to work together and cheer one another on."

Right, I thought. *This is going to be interesting.*

We clustered by lane three, ready to practice. But how were we going to be a team if Sonali wouldn't talk to either Tara or me? She avoided eye contact and so did I.

Sonali was first. Relays usually start with the backstroke in the pool, not off the starting block. Sonali jumped in and held on to the edge with her fingertips.

When the whistle blew, she pushed off hard and swam the backstroke to the opposite end of the pool, did a kick turn, and then came back.

I waited on the starting block, knees bent and arms back. *Forget everything*, I told myself, *and when you hit the water, just swim.*

The moment Sonali touched the end of the lane, I pushed off hard and dove shallow. The moment I surfaced, I swam the breaststroke as fast and as strong as I could. I reached the wall and tucked into my turn, pushed off hard, and then propelled my body down my lane toward my relay team.

"Chrissa! Go!" The cheering urged me on, though my lungs burned.

When I touched the pool's edge, Rachel dove off the block. I climbed out of the pool and cheered for her as she did the butterfly to the end and back again.

"Rachel, go!" we shouted. Finally, when Rachel touched back, Tara hit the water and swam the free-style, meaning she could pick any stroke she wanted—and like the other relay teams' anchors, she swam the crawl.

"Good times," Coach announced, "but you all can do better. In three weeks we'll have our first meet. And between now and then, the only way to improve is to practice, practice, practice."

Our team practiced until my arms and legs felt as heavy as barbells. But it gave me little time to think, and that was good. Still, I was relieved when Coach announced, "Divers, line up!"

During dives, Coach demanded absolute silence, but the moment a dive was completed, we could cheer like crazy. I quietly waited my turn in line, watching the other divers. I'd memorized the five groups of dives for springboards: forward, backward, reverse, inward, and twist. And each group had various positions: straight, pike, tuck, and freestyle. There was a whole lot more to diving than I'd imagined.

When it was Tyler's turn, he walked to the edge of the board. He circled his arms down as he pushed off the board with bent knees. Reaching for the ceiling, he soared into the air and tucked his knees to his chest; then, looking back toward the board, he found his target—the water—and dropped in headfirst.

Cheering erupted.

"What was that?" I said to no one in particular.

From behind me, Joel said, "His secret weapon! It's a reverse tuck. He's been practicing at the pool during open swim times. He wanted to surprise the team."

I couldn't believe it. If he was that determined,

maybe he really *could* go to the Olympics someday!

The coach was clapping, too. "Good effort, Tyler! Nicely executed."

"Awesome!" Tara called out to Tyler as she turned to scale the ladder next.

"That was amazing, Tyler!" Jadyn joined in, next in line.

Someone tapped my shoulder. I turned. Joel pointed two divers back. Sonali leaned closer and whispered, "Chrissa, looks like Tara and Jadyn are up to their old tricks. Acting like fans of Tyler's, just to get to you. Remember?"

I didn't reply.

"Well," she continued, "do you *really* think anything has changed?"

I replied, a little too loudly, "I don't know what to think anymore!"

"People!" Coach ordered. "Quiet!"

At the end of practice, I was determined to risk talking with Tara in the locker room. Nana's words kept going through my mind: *If you're nice to people,*

then they'll be nice to you. I needed to know if that really was true.

I changed quickly, and then walked over to where Jadyn and Tara were drying their hair by the blowers. "I need to talk," I said to Tara.

Tara flipped her hair back. "Okay. I'm done anyway." She walked away from the blower. Jadyn stepped toward us, tilting her head curiously.

"Alone, please?"

"Oh," Jadyn said, wrinkling her brow as she moved off toward her locker.

Tara followed me to my empty corner.

"Tara," I whispered, "I need to find out who sent those awful spam e-mails and posted those mean messages."

"Yeah, I saw those," she said innocently. "So did Jadyn. Wow, Coach was steaming mad, too. Think it's someone older on the team?"

"I don't know. I wondered if you knew who—"

"Why would you ask me?" She gathered her hair into a ponytail.

I didn't want to say—*because everyone knows you've been a bully*—so instead I just didn't say anything for a few seconds.

Then she met my gaze. "Chrissa, I promise—

it's not me. I'll admit that I'm a little sore about your stealing Sonali—"

"I never *stole* Sonali." Unflinching, I looked her directly in the eyes. "She makes her own decisions about friends. I don't make her do anything."

Tara glanced over her shoulder, but when she saw that no one was eavesdropping, she continued in a whisper. "Hey, here's the thing. Sonali and I used to go shopping every year for school clothes with our moms. Forever, we were best friends. Now she won't have anything to do with me."

I remembered running into Tara in the changing room at the store. No wonder she had seemed different then—softer. She was missing a tradition she'd shared with Sonali for years.

"So you didn't send a text message about me to Sonali?"

She gave me an I-have-no-idea look.

"Or 'Watch out for Chrissa, the Llama-Faced Girl'?"

"Huh?" She shook her head. "No way."

"Or the e-mails or postings this weekend?" I suddenly felt like a lawyer, cross-examining her, but I had to know.

"No. I'm telling you the truth, Chrissa. You're

going to have to take my word for it."

I wanted to, but if Tara wasn't doing this cyber-bullying, who was?

10

Ugly Messages

When I biked home with Tyler, it rained again, soaking through to my skin. I decided it was a good day to work alongside Nana in the sunroom. Organizing my craft table somehow helped me feel a little better. At least it was something I could make sense of, something I could control.

Nana and I worked quietly side by side for a couple of hours as Minnesota Public Radio played classical music in the background. I felt as if I could finally relax.

"Uh, Chrissa?"

I turned. Tyler had stepped into the sunroom. Draped around his shoulders, just like a fur wrap, lay Keefer; his eyes were closed and he purred loud enough for me to hear. "Um—you'd better come into the library and see what's online now," Tyler said quietly.

That sick feeling rushed back.

I groaned and followed him to the study, expecting to see more messages about Sonali or Gwen on the computer monitor. To my horror, a different message, complete with a photo, lit up the screen:

Ugly Messages

Who just won the Ugliest Girl in the
World contest?
You guessed it!
Chrissa Maxwell!

Alongside the message was a photo of me. It was one that had been taken last week, when a photographer came to the pool to takes pictures of everyone on the team. Mine had been cut and pasted and then blown up. Someone had altered it with black marks and added a black mustache, huge ears, a wart on my chin, and snot coming out of my nose!

Hot tears threatened.

"Who'd post that?" Tyler asked, with genuine surprise in his voice. "Must be the same person the coach said would be suspended if he caught them, huh?"

"I wish I knew who it was. I'd jail them if I could."

Tyler started cracking up. "You have to admit, Chrissa, it's pretty funny! I mean, it does sort of look like you."

"Tyler, don't start. It's *not* funny! Maybe *you* did this. You love computers."

He tried to stop laughing but couldn't. "No,

honest, I didn't. You've been pretty crabby lately, but you know I wouldn't go this far."

I broke into tears.

"Chrissa, I'm sorry." He rested a hand on my shoulder, but I pulled away. "Hey, let it go. It's just a picture. Just words."

"I've got to tell Mom and Dad," I said. "I thought I was finally okay here, but no, I'm not. And whoever is doing this, they're doing it to Sonali and Gwen, too."

I pulled on my raincoat and dashed out to Dad's pottery studio.

Dad was hunched over one of the electric pottery wheels, hands carefully pulling the sides up on a foot-high cylinder of clay. I stood near him, waiting while he finished. I knew that he couldn't just stop in the middle of throwing a pot or a vase without having the whole thing wobble. Throwing requires steady hands and tons of patience. While I waited, I hung up my dripping raincoat.

As the cylinder spun, Dad closed his hands around its top, reshaping it into an elegant vase with a narrow opening. He slowed the wheel until it stopped, and then he looked up at me.

"Hi, honey. What's up?" He reached toward my face, as if to wipe away a tear, but stopped with a quick glance at his clay-slicked hands. "Oops. Better not. Why don't you pull up a chair?"

I found a wooden stool and sat down, saying nothing.

"So—talk."

"Okay, well, I have a problem," I began, determined not to cry so that I could get through this. I told him about the text message, the mean postings on the message board, the e-mails to the team, and now this latest spam message. And I explained how Sonali and Gwen had suggested that maybe I'd done some of it.

"Ouch," he said. "This is serious, Chrissa, and I'm glad you finally came to me. I've been worried about you. I don't know that much about how these things work, but we'll talk this over with your mom as soon as she gets home, and we'll figure something out together. In the meantime"—he stood, grabbed a chunk of clay from a plastic bag, and handed it to me—"why don't you work this into something while we wait."

I didn't really feel like it, but I took the clay anyway. I slammed it down on the large wooden table and kneaded it to work out any bubbles that might be inside. Then I rolled it into a smooth gray ball. Finally I settled at the other electric wheel. I dipped a small sponge into the water basin and wet the clay, and then

I cupped my hands around it firmly as the wheel spun. When I was sure that I had centered the clay and it was turning in a perfect circle beneath my hands, I pushed my thumb into its center and began to pull outward, turning a blob of clay into—I hoped—something useful.

"It's good therapy," Dad said, working at his wheel. "Helps with thinking a problem through."

For the next hour, I was content to sit at the wheel. It calmed me down to work alongside Dad. He isn't a big talker, but I know he's there for me.

As Mom often does when she drives in, she stopped first at the studio. "Hi, Paul," she began. "And Chrissa! I didn't expect to see you here, too. Are you turning into a potter like your dad?"

"Not really, Mom," I said. "I mean, I like it, but that's not why I'm here right now." I sat back from the pot I'd just thrown and told her everything.

She tilted her head, meeting my eyes. "Oh, Chrissa honey, this is terrible! Who would do this?"

"I don't know, Mom." My voice was tinged with whining, but I couldn't stop myself. Like the hot springs we'd once visited at Yellowstone, my emotions bubbled up, ready to explode.

"Is someone other than Sonali and Gwen mad at you? Those girls from last year? Wasn't Tara, who was just over here, one of them?"

I nodded.

"Do you think she'd do that after coming over and acting like a friend?"

"I don't know." Maybe Sonali and Gwen had been right all along about Tara and Jadyn. Or could it have been Sonali and Gwen who had posted this last mean message about me? Everything was so twisted.

"Who else might be mad at you?"

"Mom!" I wailed. "I—just—don't—know!"

Then the flood that I'd been holding back broke through. I faced my wet-clay pot and sobbed.

Mom leaned over and wrapped her arms around my shaking shoulders. Her perfume sweetened the air as she pushed her cheek against mine and held me as if she wouldn't let go. "It's gonna be okay, Chrissa," she murmured. "We'll get through this together."

I appreciated her hopefulness, but I couldn't see how this nightmare would ever end. Finally, when I caught my breath again, Dad handed me a box of tissues. "Here, sweetie."

While I blew my nose and dried my eyes, my parents discussed what they knew about cyber-bullying, which wasn't much. "But it's clearly part of the same problem from last spring," Mom said. "Whether it happens online, in text messages, or face-to-face, it's still bullying. Plain and simple."

"Chrissa," Dad concluded, "we're going to put a stop to this."

"Dad, no. Please don't do—" But then I stopped myself. I was scared that whoever was behind the bully-ing might make things worse. But that *wasn't* what had happened last spring when my parents had stepped in. Things actually got better. And anyway, the way things were going, I didn't see how life could get much worse.

"This has gone too far already, Chrissa," Dad said. "As I said, I'm pretty ignorant about computers, but we'll investigate and get to the bottom of this, okay? We're here to help you stand strong and get through this."

At first I couldn't answer. My throat was all choked up again.

"Okay?" he repeated.

Though my hands were still muddy with clay, I jumped up and walked to where he sat at his wheel. Being careful not to touch his clothes, I hugged him as much as I could and whispered, "Okay."

I turned, ready to hug Mom, too.

She put up her hands and said with a laugh, "If you don't mind, I'll take my hug after you clean up and come in for dinner. I can hear your stomach rumbling, Chrissa. But it's no wonder you haven't been eating lately." She glanced at her watch. "Let's go in. Nana's probably waiting for us right now with her Monday chicken dinner."

Telling them everything must have helped. For the first time in days, I actually felt hungry.

11

Over the Edge

But in the morning, everything felt wrong again. I was exhausted from tossing and turning, tormented by that snotty-nosed, big-eared image of myself. My stomach ached. Even if we found out who was doing this, I didn't see how I could face anyone again. It was so embarrassing. Though it had helped to tell Mom and Dad, I couldn't bear going to practice today. The sender had to be someone on the team.

I pushed back the covers and made my way down to the kitchen. Mom was at the table, drinking coffee and reading the *Star Tribune*. "Mom, can we move back to Iowa?" I asked.

She patted the empty chair beside her and I sat down. "No," she said.

"Please?"

"Chrissa," she said softly, "if you run away or quit, you let the bully—or bullies—win. That's what they want."

"But, Mom, it's so awful."

"Yes, and that's why we're going to get to the bottom of this. You took the first step, Chrissa, by telling us. Now we're going to find out who's behind this."

"But Mom, I'm worried that I'll be called a tattletale." My shoulders sagged, and I didn't have the strength to lift my head to meet her gaze.

She lifted my chin and met my eyes. "You're *telling,* Chrissa, not tattling. You're doing what must be done. What's happening is not okay, is it?"

I shook my head. "No."

She kissed the top of my head. "You might feel like it right now, but you're not alone, honey. We're here for you and we're going to get through this together. I promise."

I biked with Tyler to practice, and in the locker room I avoided eye contact with everyone. I didn't know who was friend or foe, so I just kept to myself. In the pool, I concentrated on my form and my breathing. During our relay practice, I felt heavy, as if weighted down by a bag of rocks. To my amazement, I got my best time yet.

The whistle blew, and Coach called out, "Okay, swimmers! You have about fifteen minutes before the next group arrives. I'm going to be working with some of you in the shallow end. The rest of you—now would be a good time to practice anything you want—or just have a little fun."

Fun, I mused. *Now that is almost funny.* Huddling in my towel would be more fun than facing Sonali, Gwen, Tara, or Jadyn. Or was it someone else on the team?

While the diving area was empty, I hurried over to practice a dive. Above the din of voices, I bounced on the high board, and tried a forward one-and-a-half, just the way Tyler had done it at home. My body turned as I dropped, and the water sped up to meet me faster than expected, but I managed to hit the water with my hands over my head, even though my legs slapped the surface.

"Hey," Tara called out when I came up. "Are you trying to be the best girl diver at Edgewater? I thought that was *my* place."

I couldn't tell if she was mad or not.

Then she laughed. "Chrissa, I'm *joking.*"

"Yeah, don't be so thin-skinned," Jadyn added, huddled in her towel. "Can't you take a joke?"

"Really, Chrissa," Tara said. "That *was* a good try."

I swam to the edge and pulled myself up. By now Tyler and a few others were there, too, ready to dive. Sonali was on the board, and out of the corner of my eye I saw her do a nice back dive. Practicing from the swim raft all summer had made a difference.

Tyler, his hair dripping and half in his eyes,

glanced down from the ladder as he climbed to the top. "This next move is going to launch me to the Olympics," he announced. "Just watch!"

"Tyler, you're such a bragger," I called back. Then half out loud and half to myself I said, "Someone ought to teach him a lesson!"

Suddenly, Tara started up the ladder after Tyler. "I will!"

"Tara, stop! I didn't mean—"

Coach had made it clear that for safety reasons, only one person was allowed on the board and the ladder at a time.

But Tara didn't hear me. Or else she ignored me as she climbed. What in the world was she doing? She had something in mind, and suddenly I was afraid it was because of my stupid comment. Why did she have to take a simple comment and go to the extreme?

I looked for the coach, but he was busy in the shallow end. I knew I should call out to him, but I was afraid to add "tattletale" to my list of names, especially when things seemed to be going a little better with Tara.

Tyler was at the end of the board, facing the water, his body taut in concentration. I worried for him and started up the ladder after Tara, even though I knew I wasn't supposed to be on it. "Tara!" I called up. "Get off the board!"

"What?" she hissed back at me in a whisper. "I thought you said someone should teach him a lesson. I'm just having a little fun! Telling him about my cork-screw dive."

Behind me Jadyn laughed.

By the time I scrambled to the top step, Tara was partway out on the board—just as Tyler was pushing off. At that very moment, Tara jumped on the center of the board and yelled, "Corkscrew!" at Tyler.

Tyler was airborne.

His body soared up for a reverse tuck. At the full height of his dive, as he brought his knees to his chest and looked back for the board, his eyes grew wide. The double bounce had changed everything. Instead of aiming for the water, he came down crooked. His head hit the edge of the board with a terrible *whap!*

Like a puppet whose strings had been cut, he fell, flopping into the deep end.

"Tyler!" I called out, heart in my throat and sick at what I'd just witnessed. "Coach! Coach!" I screamed. "Help!"

I scrambled back down the ladder as fast as I could move.

Tyler was in the water, floating facedown.

I grabbed a pole, hoping to snag his swim trunks and drag him to the edge. But before I could remove the pole from the wall, Coach was there. He dove in. Grabbing Tyler by the shoulder, he flipped him faceup, swam with him toward the edge of the pool, and heaved him onto the concrete floor.

"Chrissa, tell the receptionist to call 911 and then call your parents!"

I returned to Tyler in less than a minute. The pool area had grown eerily quiet. Swimmers clustered around my brother. He was covered with a blanket, and his legs were elevated. I slipped closer and kneeled beside him, next to the coach. To my relief, there wasn't much blood. An ugly red egg-sized welt grew from the center of Tyler's forehead. His chest rose and fell, so I knew he was alive, but he was knocked out.

"Coach," Tara said, her face pale. "I didn't mean for anything like this to happen."

"It's my fault, too," I said, speaking up and reaching for one of Tyler's hands. "I saw what was happening and I didn't stop it."

"It was going to be a joke," Tara said.

"Sounds like you both broke rules," the coach said sternly. "Believe me, we'll deal with consequences later."

The sound of a siren loomed closer, and in moments the doors to the pool swung open. A team of medical workers hurried in. I couldn't believe they were coming for my brother. When they determined he could be moved, they eased him onto a stretcher, careful to support and then brace his head.

I wrapped my arms tightly around myself and watched them take my brother out to the ambulance. Dad's truck was just pulling up. I grabbed my shorts and jacket and ran out to meet him.

Dad spoke quickly with the medical workers and then motioned me toward the truck. "Chrissa, hop in! We'll follow."

The ambulance siren blared and its lights flashed as it pulled away from the Community Center. Dad drummed his fingers against the steering wheel as we followed close behind.

When I glanced back, I spotted Sonali and Gwen, their faces filled with concern as they waved at me.

I lifted my hand in return, grateful that they were true friends.

12

Hospital Worries

Finally, Mom stepped through the double doors of the intensive care unit. She'd turned her clinic appointments over to a resident doctor the moment Tyler entered the hospital. Now she sat down beside Nana, Dad, and me.

"Concussion," she said. "The scan shows no signs of fracture. No spinal injury. It could have been much worse. Right now they have to keep the swelling down and monitor him closely."

"When can we see him?"

"In just a few minutes. They're transferring him to a regular room now."

Once nurses had moved Tyler from intensive care to room 203, I was able to visit him. The body under the white sheets was Tyler, but I hardly recognized him. In a light blue hospital gown, he rested, a cold pack secured to his forehead. Bruising from his forehead extended toward the top of his nose and just above his closed eyes. His lips were bluish purple, and an IV line was taped to his arm.

I mustered up courage and tiptoed closer, then

bent down and kissed him on the cheek. But he didn't wake up. I fought back tears. He didn't deserve this. So what if he *had* been getting a big head about his diving? He's good. He was just excited about making progress. Maybe it was Tara's *actions* that had caused him to hit his head, but my *words*—and my fear of tattling—made me responsible, too.

"He's going to be okay," Mom said. "He's been mumbling. I expect that as the medication wears off, he's going to have quite a headache."

"Hey," he said, his voice a little gravelly.

I smiled at him, even though his eyes were closed. "Hey, Tyler."

That day, we took turns staying with Tyler. The first time Mom and Dad stepped out for a bite to eat, Nana pulled an extra set of knitting needles and yarn from her bag. "Here," she said, offering them to me. "I brought this along for you. Sometimes it helps."

Nana was right. Moving the knitting needles in and out of stitches, back and forth across rows, and transforming the orange-yellow yarn into a scarf really was what I needed. It quieted my worries and eased the ache in my heart. Most of all, just knowing that Nana understood helped more than anything.

When I got tired of knitting, I tried to play

"Brain Scan" and read Tyler's mind. I concentrated and tried to imagine what he might be thinking. But time and again my mind drew a complete blank, which scared me and filled me with worry. What if I never fully got my brother back again? He was sleeping, but I leaned over and said softly, "Here we are, brother and sister . . . and I haven't been very nice to you lately."

Nana set her knitting down on the bed and reached over to hug me. "He's going to be just fine; you wait and see. And no wonder you don't get along all the time. You're brother and sister, after all. No two people can get along *all* the time."

"But Nana, I've been mean. I've been calling him names. I've been jealous of his diving. And when he said something show-offy, I gave Tara the idea to teach him a lesson. Now look what I've done to him."

Nana seemed to search for words, but then she said, "Chrissa, you love your brother. I know that and he knows that, too. But none of us is perfect. We all make mistakes. It's how we handle our mistakes that matters. You're already admitting you made a mistake, and that's important. That takes courage. And now you can learn from it."

I sighed.

"When I was a girl," she continued, "there used

to be a saying that went, 'Sticks and stones can break my bones, but words can never hurt me.'"

"Yeah, I've heard that one."

"It isn't true, is it?"

I shook my head.

"Because words really can do a lot of damage. Once they're out there, it's hard to take them back. Then things like this can happen, even when we don't intend them to. But what's important is that we *keep* working all the time at being kind and caring, and being a good friend. And when we fail, we admit our mistakes, ask for forgiveness, and start again."

"But this isn't just a little mistake, Nana!" I whispered. "Tyler could have died."

"You're right," she said, "but what happened to Tyler is *not* your fault." She placed her hand on my shoulder and nodded. "Chrissa, it's good to know when to hold your tongue. But this? I know you didn't mean for this to happen. And neither did Tara. You probably should have spoken up, but it *was* an accident. And no doubt, hard as this is, you'll both learn plenty from it."

Later, when Nana and I went for dinner in the hospital cafeteria, the cell phone Mom had given me rang. It was Gwen. "How's Tyler?" she asked. "Sonali and I have been so worried."

"He has a concussion," I replied more calmly than I felt. "He's on medication to keep the swelling down and to keep him quiet. But he's going to be okay."

"I still can't believe it," Gwen said. "If there's anything we can do, let us know."

"Thanks."

"Um, I'm using Sonali's cell phone. She wants to talk to you, too."

"Chrissa?" Sonali began. "When you left the pool in a hurry with your dad, the coach asked us to gather your things from your locker and get them to you. I'll leave your backpack on your porch, okay?"

I sighed. "Yeah, thanks."

"Well, I'd better go," Sonali said. "We hope Tyler gets better soon. We'll call you again later, Chrissa. Okay?"

"Yeah, I'd like that."

I appreciated their phone call more than they knew.

Sometime that evening, Tyler's eyes popped open and he looked at me, all serious. "We're getting close to blastoff," he said. Then he closed his eyes again.

"Phew!" Mom said. "I know he's still a little loopy with the medication, but he's sounding more like his old self—finally!"

For the first time all night, I laughed. "Yup, sounds just like him." I felt a surge of giddiness, as if I could dance around the room and up and down the halls. But instead, I sat right on the edge of the bed beside my brother. As the minutes passed by, his babbling started to make more sense. And then, as if he was truly waking up for the first time, he kept his eyes open and blurted, "I'm really thirsty—and starving." Then he screwed up his bruised face and said, "And what am I doing *here*?" Just as quickly, he answered his own question. "Last thing I remember was the diving board. Oh . . ." He moved his hand gingerly up toward his forehead. "Wow, I think I blew that dive!"

I couldn't help myself. I planted a sisterly kiss on his cheek. "Oh, Tyler, you're right. It was going to be a 9.8, but—"

The corners of his mouth lifted slightly.

"Honestly, I'm just so glad that you're okay!"

13

Brain Scan

The next morning, after a few extra tests, Tyler was released from the hospital. On the drive home, I squeezed close to him in the backseat. There are times when he drives me so crazy that I can't get enough space between us, but just then I was so happy to have him coming home that he couldn't do anything wrong.

"I wonder if being a good diver helps when you're trying to get into the space program?" he said. "I mean, it seems like anything that helps with three-dimensional movement would be good. When you're weightless in space, you have to know where your body is in the air."

He rambled on and on, and he didn't get on my nerves a bit. That in itself was pretty much a miracle.

Later that morning, when Tyler and I played "Brain Scan" together, I guessed what Tyler was think-ing in most of my tries. When it came to colors, I got "orange" right. Maybe it was because I was thinking of the scarf I'd started, which I intended to give to Tyler. When he thought of a sport, I guessed "diving," but then, that seemed to be the only thing that Tyler had focused on all summer. And then he guessed the kind of fish I was thinking about—"pike." But of course, that's a diving position, as well as a fish common in Minnesota lakes. So maybe we really *can* read each other's minds. Or maybe, being brother and sister means that we know each other so well, we can guess, more times than not, what is in the other's mind. Either way, it felt good just to be playing a game together again.

"You know what, Tyler?" I asked.

"What?"

"You're my brother," I said, "and sometimes you bug me . . . but you're my friend, too, you know that?"

"Yeah," he said. "Same here."

After Tyler woke from a nap, Nana said he could walk with me to the barn. His forehead was bruised with shades of purple and green, but at least he didn't have to wear that ice pack all day. We leaned over the stall door while Cosmos chewed her cud contentedly and Starburst jumped and skipped around her. I wished my life were as carefree.

"Hey, you two," Dad said, entering the barn with

Mom. "We just came from a meeting with the coach, Tara's mom, and Jadyn's parents. We need to talk."

They sat down on the nearby bench. Tyler and I turned to face them.

"Three things," Mom said. "First, Chrissa, your coach has suspended both you and Tara for two weeks."

"Two weeks?" I whispered. Though I knew it was fair, my heart still sank.

"You're expected to go to practice but not to suit up. He wants you to be there in the bleachers and keeping up with what the team is doing."

"But—" I started to protest and then stopped myself. I had been on the ladder, too. And more importantly, I could have called for the coach, but I hadn't done so. "Okay."

"Second," Dad explained, "Coach Beck has been in contact with Jadyn's parents, the Johnsons, since they're computer experts. In fact, they helped him set up the swim team's message board. When we talked to your coach about the cyber-bullying, he said he'd already been in touch with the Johnsons after the first posting. They were able to find out where it's been coming from and who sent out the messages."

I held my breath, then exhaled. "Who?"

"Well, it's pretty devastating for the Johnsons as parents," Dad said. "It's their own daughter. It's Jadyn who's been doing all this."

My jaw hung limp. I turned to look at Tyler, who looked equally stunned. Jadyn? I'd never suspected her.

From their stalls, Cosmos and Checkers lifted their heads high. Their ears were alert, ready to take in the news, it seemed. Even Starburst stared at us with her big eyes.

I found my voice. "You're sure? Not Tara?"

"Not Tara," Mom repeated.

It didn't make sense. Why would Jadyn post mean messages and create hurtful images about Gwen, Sonali, and me? Jadyn was usually in the background, the one who always stood up for Tara. It just didn't add up. But then I remembered that she was good with computers.

"What do we do?" I asked. My surprise and bewilderment gave way to anger. Jadyn had no right. "What she did to us was *mean*."

Tyler elbowed me lightly. "Chrissa, you're not all that perfect, y'know. You've been calling me names all summer."

I winced.

"Okay," Mom interjected, "third. Chrissa, the

Johnsons have asked us to stop over."

"Do I have to go?" I asked. I saw no reason whatsoever to have to meet up with Jadyn after what she'd done.

"Actually," Mom replied, "though it won't be comfortable, they asked that you come along, too."

14

Techno Trouble

The last thing I wanted to do was to go to Jadyn's house. But there I was, stepping up to the brick home with its covelike entry framed with ivy. The carved sign beside the mailbox read "The Johnson Family."

I determined, from the moment we stepped inside, to let my parents do the talking. In the living room, I counted at least four computers on various counters and desks—one big-screened computer and several laptops. Computer manuals, stacks of disks, and printouts were piled everywhere.

"Please excuse the chaos," Mrs. Johnson explained with a dainty wave of her arm. She was a petite woman with tiny hands and feet. "We both work from home as computer consultants. Sometimes it's hard to know where work ends and home begins."

With a Twins baseball cap snugged on backward, Mr. Johnson rose from a computer desk. I recognized him from the meeting with the principal last spring. He grabbed his cap's rim and spun it to the front. Then he seemed to reconsider and took it off and set it on a coffee table instead.

"Thanks for coming over," he said, extending his thick hand toward my dad's in a handshake. He lowered his voice. "Daria and I create Web sites. It's our work, so Jadyn comes by her technological skills naturally. I asked you to be here so that Jadyn could apologize in person and see the impact of her actions." He nodded in my direction, but I glanced away.

Mrs. Johnson stepped toward a hallway. "Jadyn, the Maxwells are here."

A door creaked opened, and the padding of footsteps sounded in the hallway. Jaydn snugged her arms around her waist, as if the warm air had grown icy. Her gaze dropped to the wood floor.

Mrs. Johnson motioned us to the table. "Please, everyone. Have a seat." She began pouring glasses of lemonade, but no one took one.

"Jadyn," Mr. Johnson began, "I realize this isn't easy, asking you to apologize like this, but I think it's important that you try to explain your actions to Chrissa and her parents."

The silence around the table grew.

I shifted in my chair and then sneaked a look at Jadyn. She reminded me of the Wicked Witch of the West in *The Wizard of Oz*, who begins to melt into a puddle. Jadyn, who always stood up for Tara, seemed to be wilting before my eyes.

Heat crept up my neck to my face. I felt for Jadyn. I'd been fuming inside at her, but now I just felt terrible. I would die if I were in her shoes, sitting with all of us looking at her.

Jadyn's green eyes glistened as she blinked away tears. "At first, I just sent a couple of anonymous text messages? To try to get Sonali back in our group? I mean, we've been friends for years until you moved here. And then, well, over the summer Tara started to talk about how she wanted to change, to become friends with you, Chrissa, for starters. I mean, I worried I'd lose the only friend I had left." Her face reddened. "I would end up all alone!"

"What about Tara?" I asked, needing to finally know whether she had played a part. "Did she have anything to do with this?"

"She didn't know anything about it."

I felt a surge of relief. I hadn't been wrong about Tara. Tara was still Tara, jumping up the ladder at the tiniest encouragement, acting before thinking, always pushing the limits. But her wish to be friends—to change—had been sincere.

Sitting beside Jadyn, her mom leaned closer and asked, "Honey, is that why you wanted to know how to post photos on the message board?"

Jadyn flinched but then met her mother's eyes. "No and yes. At first, I just wanted to help put up team photos—kids swimming and that kind of stuff? But then, once I knew how, well, it was so easy."

At the end of the table, Mr. Johnson sat back with his arms crossed. "I thought all this ended last spring after that haircutting episode. Whatever is going on between you girls has to come to an end. We didn't raise you like this. What happened?"

Jadyn cupped her hands over her mouth and breathed through her fingers. "I'm sorry! I really am!" Tears rolled down her cheeks. "I don't know why I did it. I knew it wasn't nice, but I didn't know what else to do. Who else was going to be my friend if I lost Tara, too?"

"It's a reason," her dad said, "but it doesn't excuse the behavior. There are going to be consequences."

He shifted around in his chair, as if searching for the right words. Finally he said, "We've always said that computers are great tools, but their value depends on how they're used. They can be used for good and they can be used badly, too, as we now know all too well. Jadyn, I want you to show me everything you've put online so that we can take it down immediately. Then we'll figure out where to go from there. But first you've got some apologies to make, and you need to find a way to make it right."

Jadyn nodded. She sniffed loudly and stared into her lap. "I'm sorry?" she said, and I wondered if she meant it. Then she looked up and met my eyes. "Really, Chrissa. I mean it. I'm really sorry. What . . . what can I do to make things right?" she asked in a shaky voice.

I didn't move in my chair. After so much hurt, I wasn't sure that I was ready to forgive her. This was all happening so fast.

"I don't know. I mean, I'm not sure *what* you can do. But it's nice that you're apologizing to me."

Jadyn's shoulders shuddered and she met my eyes briefly. "Thanks."

Then I added, "Sonali and Gwen were also hurt by what you wrote. Maybe you need to apologize to them, too. That would help."

Jadyn nodded.

"Jadyn, the coach has suspended you completely for two weeks from swimming," Mrs. Johnson said, handing her a box of tissues. "You're not to go to the pool until your suspension is over."

Jadyn blew her nose. "Okay."

I wasn't happy to be suspended, either, but at

least I wasn't banned entirely from the pool. Jadyn's punishment was far more serious.

"Y'know," Jadyn's mom said to my parents, "these incidents of cyber-bullying have led me to read more about bullying of all kinds. I think that with this incident, and with all that went on last spring, it's time we put our heads together and work with the school as it deals with this issue."

"That's a great idea," Mom chimed in.

My throat was dry, and I took a long drink of lemonade while the adults talked. Although Jadyn hung her head and looked as miserable as I'd felt since the bullying had started, a wave of relief spread through me. The bullying finally had come to an end. I could breathe again.

I was smarter now. I had told the truth, asked for help, and gotten it. Maybe bullying would show up again sometime in my life, but when it did, I'd be better prepared to handle it. I had a few tricks up my sleeve. For starters, I wouldn't go it alone.

"We have e-mail access to all the parents and teachers at the school," Mr. Johnson said. "We could work with Coach Beck and Mrs. Ziminsky to see if there's any interest in gathering a few families and teachers to start brainstorming."

"Think two weeks would be too soon?" Dad asked.

Mr. Johnson shook his head. "No, why?" he asked.

"We could gather at our house for a Labor Day potluck before school starts. What do you think? It'd be a good way to start the new school year off right."

15

Looking Ahead

During the two weeks of being suspended and having to sit together on the sidelines, Tara and I got to know each other better. We cleared up some of our misunderstandings and watched Tyler as he practiced his diving moves on the floor. He was supposed to take a full month off from any activities that might risk bumping his head again, but he continued to stretch and practice as much as he could.

On the very first day of suspension, Sonali and Gwen came over before practice started. I had already apologized to both of them by phone, saying that I was sorry that I hadn't been a very good friend when they'd felt so hurt.

"We're here to apologize to *you*," Sonali said to Tara. Gwen nodded.

Tara looked surprised.

"Tara," Sonali said, twisting her hair around her finger, "we suspected *you*, not Jadyn. I guess that after last spring, we just assumed that it was you. And that was wrong. But Chrissa stood up for you and kept saying that we shouldn't jump to conclusions. That we didn't have any proof it was you."

Tara looked at me. "You did? That's really nice."

I nodded.

"Well, I guess I'm not really surprised that you suspected me," Tara said. "I know that I acted pretty bad last year—and maybe I haven't been the nicest person. But I don't want to be like that anymore. Um, would you guys accept *my* apology?"

"Maybe we should all start over," Gwen said. "If that's possible."

"For sure!" Tara exclaimed. "Why not?"

We all looked at one another, not sure what to do next.

"So," Sonali said to me, breaking the ice. "How's Starburst doing?"

"She's more adorable than ever," I replied. "You should come over and see her."

"I'd like that," she answered.

"Me, too," Gwen added. "How about today?"

I looked at Tara. "Since we can't swim here, Tara and I were going to practice swimming and diving this afternoon at home. But you're welcome to join us. It'd be fun!"

The coach blew his whistle.

"Well, we've got to go practice now," Sonali said.

"But we'll bike over later, okay?"
"Great," I said and smiled.

Summer gave us a last blast of heat, sending the thermometer soaring up to 96 degrees for our first meeting of "Safe Schools, Kind Communities."

Around 6:00, Tyler and I began greeting guests at the door. Parents, teachers, and students arrived carrying casseroles, salads, pans of bars, and bags of chips.

"What a beautiful home!"

"What a great idea!"

"Head straight through to the kitchen," Tyler said.

"Food goes on the counter," I added.

Gwen and her mom and Sonali and her parents showed up together. Sonali's mom had helped Gwen's mom find their apartment, and they'd been friends ever since.

Sonali nudged me. "I can't wait for my mom to see Starburst!" To my relief, things were much better now between us. She and Gwen had come over several times after practice to see the llamas and to swim in the lake. We'd talked out everything until it felt as if we were back to being good friends again—like before.

I braced myself for how it would be to see Jadyn after her two-week suspension from the team. Though I knew her parents were involved with the meeting, I wondered if Jadyn might stay home.

Smoke curled up from the grill as Dad cooked chicken drumsticks and hamburgers. My all-time favorite teacher, Ms. Rundell—Edgewater's art teacher—was there, too.

"What have you been working on this summer, Chrissa?" She flashed a bright smile.

"Let me show you."

First I led her to Nana's sunroom and showed her my craft table.

"How wonderful that you have your own space to work in!"

Then I led her to the pottery studio and showed her the ceramic tiles that Tara, Sonali, Gwen, and I had glazed. Each tile was painted differently, but in the center of each one was a word. One said "friendship," another said "kindness," and another said "trust." I pointed out the two I'd made—"strength" and "hello."

"Hello?" Ms. Rundell asked.

"It's the first word in a friendship," I explained.

She studied the tiles a moment longer, and then her face lighted up. "You girls have given me an idea. What if every student made a tile like this with a word that matters to him or her—a word that helps build the kind of school we want? I bet we could get the principal to give us some wall space for the project. What do you think?"

I could already see it. "I think it's great! Dad could help."

After a huge potluck dinner—with all the adults and kids at tables out on the lawn—the meeting began. Dad stepped toward a portable microphone that Coach Beck had brought for the occasion. "Thank you, everyone, for coming tonight. We've gathered as parents to work with and support the school's new anti-bullying program that starts when school resumes on Wednesday. Our job as parents, teachers, and students is to make sure the program gets launched and continues forward. Mrs. Ziminsky is here to tell us more."

People clapped. Joel whistled, two fingers to his lips. He stood with his parents and two brothers and stopped whistling only when his dad motioned to him that that was enough.

Then Edgewater's principal, Mrs. Ziminsky,

spoke about the problem and how other schools had developed plans to end bullying and make schools safer and friendlier places. "Every inch of school should be a safe zone," she said. "No student should worry about mistreatment when they enter the doors of Edgewater Elementary or when they leave."

More clapping erupted.

Next, Mrs. Johnson—Jadyn's mom—talked about cyber-bullying in particular. "You don't ever think it could be *your* child who might be the victim—or the bully." She paused. "But then it is. As parents, we need to be more involved with our kids' computer usage and take responsibility for what our kids are doing."

I looked around for Jadyn.

The meeting lasted nearly an hour, with adults and even a few kids sharing their ideas. Near the end, Tyler and I passed out bookmarks that we'd helped design, print, and cut. Sonali, Gwen, and Tara had helped, too, by gluing dried summer flowers onto each one before we laminated them. And then we'd tied a tassel of yarn that had come from our own llamas. They were works of art! To my surprise, I noticed Tara and Jadyn sitting together at the far table, side by side, with Tara's mother, whose hair always looked Hollywood perfect. I walked over to them. Though Tara and I were becoming friends, I was glad that she hadn't abandoned Jadyn. "Here you go," I said, handing them bookmarks.

"Thanks," Tara replied. "Gee, they look great!"

I smiled back. "They should—you helped. Um, hi, Jadyn," I added. "I'm glad you're here."

She drew in an uneasy breath and nodded.

Then together, everyone was asked to stand and read the words on the bookmarks. Our voices floated over the warm summer evening, blending with the song of crickets and seagulls. We read:

> *I promise to be kind to others,*
> *and to treat others*
> *as I wish to be treated.*
> *I promise that when I witness mistreatment,*
> *I will speak out against it.*
> *If I hurt someone with my words or actions,*
> *I will sincerely apologize and*
> *make it right with that person.*

After the formal part of the meeting was over, Tyler and I helped serve strawberry shortcake topped with swirls of whipped cream. While the parents visited over coffee, kids spread out across the lawn.

To help keep away mosquitoes, Dad lit torches and started a bonfire. A few kids changed into swimsuits and played along the sandy shore.

"Hey," Tyler suggested to some of us older kids, "let's play cards!"

Gwen, Sonali, Joel, and I joined Tyler in the gazebo. I shuffled the deck until I was certain the cards were completely mixed and ready for a new game.

Tyler, who barely showed signs now of having hit his head, looked over his shoulder and whispered, "Hey, look who's over there." He looked right at me, and in a Brain-Scan moment, I knew who he was talking about before even looking. I turned.

Tara and Jadyn wandered a few yards from the gazebo. They gazed at the younger kids working on sand castles but seemed uncertain of what to do or where they fit in.

I waved them over. "C'mon, you two! We're just starting a new game."

They brightened and headed our way. I handed the deck of cards to Tyler, unfolded two more chairs, and pulled them over to the table.

"You're sure?" Jadyn asked.

"Absolutely," Tyler replied, dealing cards one by one across the table. Jadyn sat directly to his left.

For a few seconds, Jadyn and Tara were silent as they picked up their cards and sorted them.

"Thanks for including us," Jadyn said as she played her first card.

Tara nodded her head as she looked at her cards. "Yeah, thanks. But I better warn you, I'm pretty good."

"Ah, but you—" Tyler said grandly, "—haven't yet faced the Defender of the Galaxy!"

Joel boomed, "Brace yourselves for defeat!"

"Uh-oh," I said, with an exaggerated sigh. "Here we go again!"

Outside the gazebo, the bonfire illuminated the gathering shadows. In chairs beside the fire, Mom visited with other mothers. Nana carried Starburst in her arms, to the obvious delight of younger children.

Our laughter rose from the gazebo and carried across Lake Chandler.

I couldn't have hoped for a better beginning to fifth grade.

Dear Readers,

As Chrissa discovers, there are ways to stand strong and put an end to bullying—but it isn't always easy. Standing strong works best when you have friends and family to support you, and when your school and community take a stand against bullying.

But the more we talk about bullying, the more we can stop it. Speak out if it's happening to you— or if you see it happen to others. And be sure to let adults know what's going on.

Chrissa's stories were inspired by letters from real girls, just like you. We've included some letters on the next few pages. Think about your own story as you read them. You can also keep the conversation going by finding others who have read the Chrissa books and talking about her story. If you need help getting started, use the questions on pages 122 and 123 to begin the discussion.

Most important, keep talking. Keep trying. Together we will make a difference.

Your friends at American Girl

Picked On

Dear AG,

All the kids pick on me because I'm different.
They say I have cooties and call me names.
I keep getting the same advice: "Just ignore it."
"Laugh and pretend it's funny." Can you give
some different advice?
—Not Laughing

What these kids are doing is wrong and cruel. With teasing this mean, an adult should get involved. You should talk to your parents, and together, you should go to the teacher or principal. Above all, don't let these kids make you feel bad about yourself. Find things that you love to do and put your heart into doing them. A lot of creative, talented people were picked on for being "different" when they were kids. In truth, our differences are what make us interesting. Try hard to be proud of the girl you are, and remember that it's the girls who are true to themselves who will be the happiest in the end.

Honesty

Dear American Girl,
One of my friends lives very close to me.
We visit each other a lot—almost every day.
Usually we have fun, but lately it's getting
boring. The problem is that I don't know
how to turn her down. I'm afraid I'll hurt
her feelings if I tell her the truth!
—Bored but can't admit it

Just because you live close to someone doesn't mean you have to spend every day together. It's okay to let your friend know that you have other things to do. The key is to say it in a way that isn't hurtful. Try something like, "Today isn't good. How about tomorrow?" Or "I have stuff to do today—are you free on Saturday?" As long as you are nice about it, she should understand.

But *maybe* you and your friend just need to get creative. Let her know in a nice way how you're feeling, and then suggest something like a trip to the library to look up new projects or games to try. With a little effort, you might get the good times rolling again!

To: American Girl
From: Divided
Subject: Choices

Dear AG,
I have a new friend here at school. My other friends don't like her. They say they won't be my friends if I hang out with her. What should I do?

You are being bullied and you should stand up for yourself. If you let others make decisions for you, you won't feel in charge of your life, and it's doubtful that you will be happy. Instead, let your friends know that you'll be making your own choices. It may be hard at first, but down the road, you'll be glad you listened to your heart.

On and Off

Dear AG,

This girl and I have been friends for most of our lives. We do the same things, have the same opinions, and even wear the same clothes! But lately, we have been fighting a lot and sometimes we are so mad that we don't talk to each other. We do apologize eventually but always end up in another fight. I can't deal with this on-and-off thing. What should I do?

—Confused

Friendship is like a dance. Sometimes you're closer and sometimes farther away. Just because you have a long history with this girl does not mean that you have to be together all the time. It doesn't even mean that you'll be lifelong friends. People—and friendships—change over time. Maybe the two of you need to agree to step back a bit, give each other some space, and then see how it goes from there. Good luck!

BFF Bully

Dear American Girl,
I have a best friend, and we do everything together. Last night we had a sleepover and she told me that if I want to be her real BF, I would have to take a test! I said I would think about it, and now she is really mad. HELP! I'm not sure what to do.
—Wondering

It sounds as if your friend is trying to control you, and control in a friendship is *never* a good thing. In healthy relationships, you don't have to "prove" yourself. You were right to tell her you would think about it. Let her know that while you want to be her friend, your word and your friendship will have to be enough.

Making It Right

Dear AG,
I used to be great friends with a girl when we were in third grade, but when she started hanging out with someone else I got angry. I sent her nasty messages and was awful to her. Now we're going into sixth grade, and I want to be friends again—but how? Is it too late? Should I try? Please help!
—Sorry

Yes, you should try. Start by talking to her. Admit your mistakes from the past, apologize, and ask her if you can be friends again. Even though what happened between you seems like ancient history, it may take some time for this girl to feel comfortable around you again, so be patient. If it doesn't work out, at least you'll know that you did what you could to make things right.

Discussion Questions

1. The term *cyber-bullying* is used throughout the book. What is cyber-bullying? Have you known anyone affected by it? What do you think should be done about this problem? Can you think of some ways to stop cyber-bullying? (pages 64, 71, 78, 95, 103, 110)

2. There are references to "stealing friends" in this story. What is meant by "stealing" a friend? Can friends really be "stolen"? If so, how does it happen? If not, what *can* be blamed for changes in a friendship? (pages 3, 70)

3. Chrissa wants to give Tara a second chance at being friends, but Gwen and Sonali aren't so sure. Does everyone deserve a second chance? What would you do in this situation? (pages 12, 21, 47)

4. Chrissa wonders if Tara is influencing her. Can friends or others influence our behavior? Have you ever found yourself acting differently around a friend? Was it a problem? If so, what should you do about it? (pages 42, 54, 63)

5. Chrissa wants to tell her parents what's going on, but she doesn't. Later, when she does talk to them, things get better. Why do you think she waited? Is it hard to talk to grown-ups? What can adults do to make it easier to talk to them? (pages 61, 75–78)

6. Chrissa worries about being a "tattletale." At the pool, she knows that what Tara is doing is wrong but she doesn't stop it—and Tyler ends up hurt. What is the difference between *telling* and *tattling?* Do you think it was fair that Chrissa got in trouble for not telling? Why or why not? (pages 81, 83–86, 88, 95)

7. Jadyn tries to explain why she bullied the other girls online. What do you think Jadyn should have done instead? Have you ever done something you regret? Were you able to "make it right" with the people involved? (pages 100–102)

8. Jadyn's parents and the Maxwells take steps to support an anti-bullying program being developed at the school. How do you think a school program could help? What could you do to make a difference in your school? (pages 103–104, 107–114)

Meet the Author

Mary Casanova has published more than twenty books, including *Chrissa, Jess,* and *Cécile: Gates of Gold,* also for American Girl. To write *Chrissa Stands Strong,* she tapped into her own childhood memories, as well as drawing on her experiences as a parent of two children who are recently graduated from college. She and her husband live in northern Minnesota, where they ride their horses, Midnight and JJ, and explore Rainy Lake and Voyageurs National Park with their two dogs.